I WANT MY
OWN BRAIN

ISBN-13: 9798388539304

Kindle E-book Edition April 22,2015
Smashwords E-book Edition Nov. 10, 2011

Cover design by: Lorraine Ray
Printed in the United States of America
Published in Tucson, Arizona 85716

To Mike and Julie.

I WANT MY OWN BRAIN

Lorraine Ray

Stephanie Falls nibbled her toast into an interesting oblong and listened, without comprehending, as her parents discussed the various effects of the wind that had scoured their yard since midnight. Sometime before dawn—neither parent knew exactly when—a large palm frond had crashed onto the roof of the carport next door, and as they ate their breakfasts the next morning they watched old Mrs. Webster, in polka-dotted gloves and a velour track suit, clamber onto a stepstool in front of her carport. Mrs. Webster's home was built on land that sloped toward an arroyo, and the Falls' kitchen window overlooked the roof of her carport. Together, Mr. and Mrs. Falls and Stephanie, watched as Mrs. Webster's eerie gloves groped blindly for the big palm leaf. The Falls discussed the rigid precision of their neighbor's yard and how their own modest pink adobe pleased onlookers without garish, old-fashioned, colored gravel. With satisfaction at this minor superiority over Mrs. Webster, who was a relentless busybody, Mr. and Mrs. Falls scraped their last spoonfuls of yogurt out of their cups and then panicked when a horn blared outside.

"I hope that's not our cab," said Mr. Falls, his voice rising with nervous tension as he leaned toward the window. He brushed the curtain aside and scanned the front of the house beyond the cactus hedge and a low pink wall. "It's Roadrunner Rendezvous!" he exclaimed.

"Oh my god," said Mrs. Falls in a tired voice. She rose to check the window herself and, then said, "I'll get the luggage. Go greet him or he might leave without us."

While Mr. Falls carried his empty yogurt cup around the table several times and then ran out to the curb, leaving the front door wide open so that dust and dried Bermuda grass could freely fly in, even onto the wood of the living room floor, something Stephanie had never, ever seen, her mother dashed back and forth to the kitchen enough times to cram a jar of jelly and the butter into the refrigerator door and the dishes into the sink. She also grabbed their bags from the hall, and came back to find Stephanie unmoved, alone at an empty table, still munching a somewhat smaller oblong of toast. Stephanie, who was eight, but small for her age, was effectively hidden by her chair. "Come on," urged her mother, grasping her wrist and pulling her gently.

"Your cab came early, didn't it!" screeched Mrs. Webster over the wind. Gloating over their troubles, Mrs. Webster stood on her manicured gravel side yard as Stephanie and her mother came out their front door. She held the great, glossy-brown palm frond upright beside her like a hideous club and squinted in the intense morning sunshine. Behind her, far away, like some stagey, painted backdrop, a desert mountain wore a thick band of tan, a grimy ribbon of dust.

"Yes, yes," said Mrs. Falls irritably.

"And you say you don't need your mail picked up?" called Mrs. Webster, feigning neighborly concern.

"It's not necessary, Mrs. Webster," said Mrs. Falls, locking the front door. "My parents live in town and they can swing by. You met them once, remember?"

"Hmm," said Mrs. Webster suspiciously, as though she didn't believe most people she met were really who they said they were. "Maybe I did, ah-huh, maybe so. But listen, if I were you, I'd cancel this trip to Mexico. It was all right some years ago, if you liked rustic vacations, and maybe the worst that would happen to you down there would be some soured refried beans. But now? The place is swarming with drug lords," she said.

"Our plans are definite," said Stephanie's mother.

"You're smart to leave the little one here then, at least," she called, but her demeanor showed she didn't think Mrs. Falls was ever very smart.

At this, Stephanie stopped frowning at the horrid Mrs. Webster. She concentrated her full disapproval on her mother. Her parents' trip wasn't news, but during the night Stephanie had forgotten. Just before bed Stephanie's mother had mentioned, again, the big terrible fact—that her parents were leaving for a second honeymoon in Mazatlán and she wasn't going with them.

"Goodbye, Mrs. Webster!" said Mrs. Falls. She hustled Stephanie toward the cab and whispered: "Granny Hilda will be there to pick you up after school, but if she isn't, go to the office and tell them she's picking you up and they should call her. They know everything, but just in case. I don't trust that office manager. She acts like she's taking things down when I talk to her, but most of the time she gets stuff wrong."

Stephanie's shock was absolute and all

encompassing. The idea of having to stay alone with her grandparents for an entire weekend stupefied her. The whole thing was so unjust that she couldn't figure out how she ought to start complaining.

"Goodbye!" screamed Mrs. Webster as the sliding door of the cab closed. "Hope I see all of you on Monday!"

The city traffic moved quickly in the cool and windy desert morning. On their way to the airport, they ordered the cab to stop at the open gate in Stephanie's schoolyard beside a blighted lemon tree and a leafless pomegranate bush. With its dark archways and thick adobe walls, Stephanie's school had masqueraded as a Spanish mission for forty years. The early sunlight warmed the tan plaster of those walls where a boy in a wool cap leaned backwards and blew into his cupped hands. In the early morning sun, his shadow on the wall stretched toward the cab with spidery arms.

The van door slid open, dust blew in along with bright yellow sunshine, and Stephanie's father lifted her out and set her on the dirt parkway. "There you go, Pumpkin. Love yah," he said. "Have a great day and learn a lot!"

A morose Stephanie said nothing in response, but she scuffed toward the monitor who was a big woman in dark glasses with a walkie-talkie and an attitude. Stephanie tried to hang around outside the chain link fence after her mother blew a kiss and the van door banged closed, but the monitor would have no part of that, and called her in behind the fence, and sent her shuffling glumly toward the playground. As the cab pulled away, her mother felt a guilty pang to see Stephanie drop her eyes to the ground rather than acknowledge her mother's nervous goodbye wave. During breakfast Stephanie's buttery fingers had met up with her short brown hair, but no one had done anything about the resulting mess atop her head.

"Her friends are going to show up soon," said Mrs. Falls, scanning the empty schoolyard from the van window, "I know it's an awfully cold, windy morning, and she's really mad at us, but why does she have to look so miserable? And why did the only flight to Mazatlán have to leave so early?"

"She'll be fine," Mr. Falls said.

"Oh, yeah, jeez. I'm beating myself up for nothing."

"She'll have a wonderful day and a great weekend," said Mr. Falls.

"Well, I know Mom will take good care of her," added Mrs. Falls quietly.

"And your dad. He just dotes on her."

Mrs. Falls cheered up considerably at this remark. "Isn't he getting silly about his little snickerdoodle?" she asked.

Her husband nodded. "Yeah, he's crazy about her. He's got to stop feeding her so much ice cream, though."

"I feel bad leaving her. Tell me that nothing much is apt to happen in a few short days," said Mrs. Falls.

"Nothing much is apt to happen in a few short days. There, happier?"

"A little bit, maybe. Oh, I forgot. Mom mentioned something last night. About Helen. There's some kind of problem. With her classes. She's sort of depressed or something and she might be staying over, too. I don't know. Maybe that's good?"

"Oh? What?" asked Mr. Falls.

"Helen wants to drop out of school, I guess. She's upset. She thinks she made a mistake about graduate school and she might be staying over with Mom and Dad."

"Graduate school, *pppfffttt*," said the cabbie from the front seat, inserting himself in the conversation, "My brother-in-law—he flunked out of a graduate program—Arid Studies! Now he owns a nice organic farm. Out in the country near Rio Rico. He's not gonna push himself anymore."

"My days in graduate school were the happiest in my life," said Mr. Falls.

"You chose well. Everybody knows what a lawyer does, but what exactly is economics?" said Mrs. Falls.

"Oh, economics is it then?" continued the cabbie knowingly. "That's it. That explains it. No one knows what that is. Economics. That's bullshit, that's what that is."

A startled Mrs. Falls processed the cab driver's harsh assessment during the time it took them to pass a large parcel of land covered with lacy creosote bushes, which were waving frantically in the wind. Mrs. Falls wondered when she saw Helen again if she would be disloyal to claim that economics was bullshit (not that she was forming her opinions based on what some random cabbie had said to her, of course) or if she should tone that down a bit. Maybe it would be better to say nothing, to make no comment of her own and wait and see what her sister said about it. She thought she ought to criticize economics since her sister had been feeling low about herself since she'd entered graduate school, but she would have to take her sister's lead. Then, thinking about her conversation with her mother, Mrs. Falls remembered she had forgotten to tell her husband that her father was still insisting on marching as a mountain man that weekend, in a parade, but the plan was to include Stephanie.

"Oh, I forgot to tell you. On Sunday Stephanie gets to march in a parade dressed up as a mountain man, or I should say, girl. Up in the mountains in that parade Dad talked about? The one he wanted us to go to?"

Mr. Falls laughed in relief. "Well, we haven't got a thing to worry about then. If Stephanie gets to dress up in a stinky old suede suit and march in a parade, she'll soon forget us. Hey, come to think of it, hasn't she been talking about something she's doing in school this week?"

"Oh? I don't know," said Mrs. Falls, surprised and relieved. "Was there something? I don't think so. Something different?"

"There was something," said Mr. Falls. "Ah, I'm not sure what it was. Something she really liked."

"I don't know what ... what was it? Dancing?" asked Mrs. Falls.

"That's it! Dancing!"

"Square dancing! Yes, they're learning that in school. They do that every year. You're right, Stephanie loves it."

And it was square dancing later that day that completely cheered Stephanie up so that she was lifting her knobby knees in time to the squawky beat kept by the fiddlers on the CD, *Silver Star over Arizona* by The Pioneer Pinetoppers. Minutes remained before she would complete the day in second grade, and in those minutes, Stephanie executed her best do-si-do while crossing her arms on her chest resolutely, the way her teacher, Mrs. Bowden, had taught the class during strenuous square dance lessons that week. Then, just when Stephanie had snapped back in her place, the caller, who was none other than Mrs. Bowden herself using a pink wireless microphone, shouted "Ladies and Gents, Boys and Girls, promenade your partner!"

Stephanie performed the promenade, letting only two of her fingers touch the palm of that boy named Dylan, who was her partner, and who happened to be sort of exasperating, actually. She knew him to be the kind of boy who drew ridiculous space battles with aliens in the margins and on the backs of all his school papers, and now she knew he was also the type who didn't lift his knees high enough during the do-si-dos and who promenaded with a silly lope. Yet, despite his deficiencies, Stephanie was rather glad when together they swept along with the big circle of children in the clearing of desks, swept by the computers and the listening center, but unfortunately swept faster and faster and far too near the gray metal wastepaper basket beside Mrs. Bowden's desk, which received a kick from Stephanie's foot and toppled with a thundering clatter.

The various balls of spoilt paper that the children had generated that day, the misspelled words and the disastrous arithmetic alike, spilled out and rolled like tumbleweeds over the old green linoleum floor of the schoolroom. Stephanie and Dylan do-si-doed around them, giving them kicks and laughing wildly, and most of the other kids, who initially looked on with horror at what Stephanie and Dylan were doing, joined in on the fun, kicking and stomping the papers even as Mrs. Bowden stopped calling the square dance, let the microphone flop against her chest, and pressed her eyes closed.

When her eyes opened again, which was not quickly, her face had clouded. She heaved her considerable girth closer to the small CD player, bent over it, and punched the pause button. "Square dancers. Ladies and gentlemen. Boys and girls. What do you think you are doing?" Her voice projected a creepy anger over the room.

The laughing children went silent and still.

"Square dancers. May I remind you that square dancing is a privilege, and not a right, and there are many other children who wish that they were doing square dancing right now instead of their mathematics," Mrs. Bowden said. She broke this sentence into short phrases that rose into a thundering crescendo. "What do you think you're doing with all these shenanigans!" Just then the door to the bathroom swung open and a boy blundered out, but the instant he saw Mrs. Bowden's angry face, and the children frozen in apprehension, he dove back in, developing an urgent concern for the state of his unwashed hands.

"Pick up every single one of those messy papers," Mrs. Bowden ordered. The dutiful children ran around the room picking up wastepaper. Stephanie snatched one piece away from a boy and stuffed it down his shirt. Mrs. Bowden saw this, and felt herself boil over. She found Stephanie Falls to be an especially exasperating and irritating child.

"Stephanie, I want you of all people, someone new to the Seahorse Classroom, to stop these shenanigans! Turn your card."

On her way to the behavior chart to change her green card to yellow, Stephanie was momentarily chastised. What had she meant by what she had done? She didn't remember exactly, except that knocking the can over was an accident, and then the rolling paper looked fun to kick, and the boy's neck looked like a good place to stuff some paper. She was sorry about doing shenanigans in Mrs. Bowden's room. Stephanie, however, specialized in shenanigans and she wasn't able to stop them.

A few minutes later, when the school bell went off with a horrid sound, something like *rrrattterchrattt,* Mrs. Bowden lined them up and admonished them not to run in the halls and to go home their ordinary way. Then, Mrs. Bowden let them past her and out the door. Stephanie did not get a sticker (because her card was yellow) though she doubted her mother would notice the difference, and then, just when she was thinking about her mother not noticing the sticker, which you were supposed to get if you were good all day, and which she had never yet received in three weeks in the Seahorse classroom, Stephanie noticed the tall figure of her grandmother, Granny Hilda, standing under the ramada near a towering Eucalyptus tree, in the place where her mother should have been.

It was a horrible sight for Stephanie. Actually, no logical explanation for it occurred to Stephanie for quite some time. Halfway to Granny Hilda, Stephanie was forced to remember the unpleasant fact she had learned again that morning which was her parents' Mazatlán trip, and the fact that her grandmother was taking Stephanie to her home, the big mansion in El Encanto, the one she shared with Grandpa Drummond.

Granny Hilda, a white-haired woman with bulgy gray eyes, had a worried look on her face as she scanned the crowd of kids crossing the dusty, hard-packed Bermuda grass on the school playground. It looked as though she were being shipped off to a school for the first time with unsuitable luggage—that little new suitcase Stephanie's mother had given Stephanie for her eighth birthday which said "You Can Be a Star" on the side of it. It had some smaller print claiming it was "for girls on the go." Stephanie had only used the case for swimming parties before, never for an overnight case, which was a certain compensation for having to spend a couple of nights in a creepy old house with a pair of grandparents whom you hardly knew. Stephanie also thought she probably was a girl on the go now, and that might not be a bad thing when your parents were evil enough to abandon you at eight years of age.

As Stephanie walked toward the ramada, Granny Hilda noticed that Stephanie's shoulders had squared up with the width of her hips in the way they do when a child is eight and her face had changed so that she no longer resembled her father, but instead favored a great-grandmother on Hilda's side named Eustace Epping, except with one new front tooth as crooked and lonesome as a ghost town tombstone jutting out over her bottom lip. It was hard for Hildegard to remember ever being young enough to have had only one front tooth and to have shown her emotions so prominently on her face. Stephanie looked horrified to see Granny Hilda there instead of her mother. Of course, Hildegard had had two brothers and three sisters, a situation which brought with it its own inconveniences, but if your parents went away and you had to stay with your grandmother and grandfather at least there were lots of other kids with you for protection and comfort.

She handed Stephanie her suitcase. "Did

you remember I was coming to pick you up?" Granny Hilda asked Stephanie.

"Oh, yeah, sure," Stephanie mumbled. "I member everything. Just tell me anything and I'll member it for you."

They walked together across the Bermuda field, through the same gate in the fence Stephanie had gone in in the morning, to Hilda's shiny brown SUV. When Stephanie got in on her side, Granny Hilda started talking. "Now, Stephanie, I just wanted to tell you about a little thing, uh...a little issue that has come up. It's something, something a little bit surprising which happened yesterday. It doesn't have anything to do with your parents in Mazatlán or you, really. What it does have to do with is your Aunt Helen. Aunt Helen is going to be staying at the house this afternoon and maybe all the weekend. She's at home with your grandfather right now. He's watching her. Doing his best to keep an eye on her while I pick you up."

"What do you mean, Granny?" asked Stephanie as she braced the suitcase on her knees and popped the locks open and shut continuously like gunfire. "Why does Grandpa Drummond have to stay with Aunt Helen and watch her?"

"It's nothing important, really," said Granny Hilda in an unconvincing manner.

Stephanie stopped playing with the

suitcase lock and thought for a moment. "Wow!" she exclaimed, "maybe I can play with her all weekend!"

"Now, now, Stephanie," said Granny Hilda in a frightened voice, "that's exactly what I don't want you to...uh...what I wanted to talk to you about. I don't want you to think your Aunt Helen is over at our house to play with you. Not at all! In fact, you're going to have to get that idea completely out of your head. Helen being there doesn't mean she's going to be able to play with you all weekend. It's just a bad circumstance, that's all. Aunt Helen is kind of...unhappy like...and I think you're old enough, my goodness, you're almost nine aren't you, in nine months you'll be nine years old, think of it, and you're going to have to understand. Everyone, including Aunt Helen, has only recently found out that she's a little unhappy. You could say her feelings are a little delicately arranged."

"Huh? Whaddaya mean?" asked Stephanie, squinting at her grandmother.

"Well, what I mean to say is that she might look sad and strange this afternoon. That's what you're going to notice when we get home. You're going to notice Aunt Helen looking strange and a little bit sad, far off, like something is bothering her, but you won't be able to tell what's bothering her, and I don't want you to say anything like 'you look strange and sad, Aunt Helen.' Can you promise me that?"

"Uh, okay, I guess," said Stephanie. "I can sometimes not say stuff. Or say stuff. I can say 'I'm really, really sorry' when I hate someone. Stuff like that." Stephanie sniffed importantly.

"All right then. I think you can do that. In fact, I'm sure of it, because you are a big girl now. Almost nine years old. And Helen just needs a little quiet time to herself. She doesn't need to see a special doctor," Granny Hilda explained, "it isn't that serious of a problem. These kinds of problems go away, I think, when the stress is gone. To make her see a doctor would be making a mountain out of a molehill. Everyone is entitled to have a problem in their life and not be brought to a doctor. She needs to sort herself out. She's made the decision she needed to make, dropping out of graduate school, and now all she needs is people to leave her alone for a few days and she'll get better."

"I'll help her," said Stephanie, getting into the spirit of the problem.

"Now, Stephanie. I told you before what's wrong with Aunt Helen isn't anything that you can help; you should let Aunt Helen take care of herself."

Stephanie studied Granny.

Granny Hilda tried an analogy. "Your Aunt

Helen is like a sunken boat. Let's let her right herself. Let her come bubbling up happily on her own, okay?"

Stephanie frowned. She hadn't noticed this cruel streak in her grandmother before. Stephanie pointed out some facts: "Granny, every time a boat in my bathtub sinks, it doesn't do anything to come up by itself! If I sink one of them, it lies around at the bottom of the tub until the water's drained. And Daddy has to come back in later and shake it out and set it on the side of the tub for me."

"Ah, well, I see that's not going to work, so let's don't think too much about toy boats anymore," Granny Hilda replied. "Boats aren't what we're talking about. We're talking about people. I don't even know how we got off onto that topic, actually. It's Aunt Helen we're talking about. Aunt Helen doesn't want to take courses in economics anymore she wants to—"

"Eeka what?" asked Stephanie.

"Eh...it doesn't really matter, dear. The point is she really feels very sad about what she had been doing for the last years —studying eeka—studying and she can't take studying anymore for the rest of her life. She is fed up with it. This is a bad time for her. A personal crisis, a turning point in her life."

"Yeah, I hate school, too," said Stephanie. "I've about given up on it. I don't even want any of those stickers. Ms. Bowden can keep them."

"Maybe she has wasted a few years of her life," Granny Hilda went on, ignoring Stephanie, "so that's bound to make her upset. No one can look back and realize their mistakes without feeling a bit unhappy, you see, and it certainly isn't anything to worry about, oh no, absolutely not, because it happens to the best of families and I'm a mother who has seen her fair share of troubles...yes, I have. It's making a mistake that's wearing on her, that's all, and it's troubling her thoughts today, though she ought to be better tomorrow. I dare say she will be. She is not making a lot of sense when she talks or in the way she's acting around the house, though, Stephanie, you should make no comments, all right."

In this, Granny was repeating herself.

"Got that," said Stephanie coldly.

"From now on," Granny Hilda explained, "Aunt Helen will want to do other things besides studying economics, and the most important other thing she wants to do now is art, well, painting, actually. Oil painting in a very modernistic style. We must all make it as easy as possible for her to do painting and for her not to think about what she used to do. It had been crushing for her to realize that all she ever wanted to do was painting," Granny Hilda said, "and we all have to try and understand and not make things uncomfortable for her by bothering her or stopping her or asking her questions. You can help. You aren't to ask Aunt Helen what is the matter or pester her."

Stephanie protested. This was the third time that she had been told the same thing! What did Granny think of her? That she was stupid? "I never pestered her! I never did that!" exclaimed Stephanie angrily.

Granny Hilda agreed that pester was probably not the best word to use, but that she would simply have to leave Aunt Helen alone or with an adult, perhaps with, Granny, Grandpa Drummond, or Uncle Will, Helen's husband, if he could get back from his rocket testing. Also, the weekend was going to be doubly stressful because Grandpa Drummond wanted to join his mountain man group for a parade and that would complicate everything.

"Playing is what she needs," said Stephanie adamantly.

"No," Granny Hilda disagreed, "I know playing sounds like a good thing to you. It probably sounds like what would make Aunt Helen happier. That's good thinking on your part and very kind of you, too, but in this case I'm afraid it won't do. I don't want you to bother Aunt Helen about playing. It won't be right, Stephanie, because what might make a child happy will not help an adult. Our needs are different. Oh, it would be a hard thing for me to explain the needs of an adult to an eight-year-old," Granny Hilda sighed, "that would take more time than what we have now, during the drive home. The best thing to say about it is that your Aunt Helen needs time alone to think about difficult things—adult things—things a little girl like you can't really understand."

L ater that same afternoon, Stephanie slumped in the bay window of her grandparents' library and watched her Aunt Helen drift by outside on the grassy expanse of the garden lawn. Drift by once more, that is, because she had already drifted by five or six times since Stephanie had been sitting there. This time her aunt was closer, the shadow that came first on the lawn was nearly life-sized, and when Aunt Helen herself strolled by the window, Stephanie could see her aunt's sour expression, an expression just like she had licked a palm-full of that lime chili powder, Loco Lemon, that was so popular with the kids at her school.

Aunt Helen paced the lawn with her left

hand clutching her right arm at the elbow, and with this right arm held stiffly at her side. Aunt Helen's shoulders hunched high; they rode up near her ears. She was pale and skinny, skinnier than Stephanie remembered her being before, when Stephanie had previously thought her aunt was about as skinny as a person could ever get. Was anything drawing her attention inside? To Stephanie? Stephanie hoped not. She liked her Aunt Helen, but all this pacing around was rather weird. It was painful for Stephanie to admit that her aunt might be a First-Class, A-Number One, Weird-o Person. Admitting this was horrible, especially since Aunt Helen, age twenty-three, was the youngest person Stephanie was going to have near her for the next three days and Stephanie wanted desperately for her aunt to play.

For two whole hours after she had arrived at her grandparents' home, she had played with Grandpa Drummond. What an awful experience that had been! He had not let her change some little mistakes she made at the board games, and he made her read the entire instructions to chess aloud—with him correcting her reading mistakes—before they could even set the horses and castles on the board. And he kept calling her 'his little snickerdoodle' and teasing her. He asked for the names of her boyfriends, who he said he wanted to call. Stephanie thought he was some kind of fiend, probably, about that boyfriend thing. She didn't want to remember how awful playing with her grandfather had been.

The ominous tick of a black ormolu clock on the mantelpiece above the fireplace mocked Stephanie's thumping heart. Should she go outside and play with Aunt Helen, she wondered? Was Aunt Helen in a good mood walking around out there that way? Somehow, looking at her aunt, that didn't seem very likely.

During their discussion on the way home from school, Granny Hilda had made a big deal about how Stephanie ought to leave Aunt Helen alone as much as possible because she had something important to do. Hmmm, thought Stephanie, was walking past the library windows over and over again with one arm holding the other one down the important thing Aunt Helen needed to do? If so, Stephanie didn't think her Aunt Helen was doing it with much style. Stephanie thought almost anyone who was hardly trying at all could walk by the windows better than what Aunt Helen was doing; the whole performance was a big mess, really. Aunt Helen barely turned her head when she got next to the windows. A better way to walk by any window, in Stephanie's opinion, would be to walk right around the lawn and come up slyly, though acting perfectly normal, until you were right near the windowsill. Then, just as you crossed in front of the glass, you should pull down your lower eyelids and roll up your eyes at whoever was inside, like you were some kind of freak, or you thought they were, and then you should run off to a spot behind the nearest bush. Dense, leafy bushes grew against the garden wall near the gate. Perhaps she really ought to go out and show Aunt Helen what she could do with the remaining hours of the day?

But no, Stephanie remembered Granny Hilda had said Aunt Helen needed to be alone; consequently, Stephanie thought the best job for her now was to make sure that no one who might be planning to disturb her aunt lurked in Grandpa Drummond's library.

Stephanie took it upon herself to creep toward the big, overstuffed couch and pounce upon it as though she suspected some demon intruder was crouching behind it. She peeked over the back. At nothing.

Crossing the room quickly, she tipped over a large basket to see if anyone had gotten in there when she wasn't looking, but the contents consisted solely of air and with that secured, she began to worry about the windows and she yanked back the pair of flowery curtains covering the French doors.

"Ah-ha!" she cried at the sight of the big empty yard outside. In the middle of the huge lawn a tiled fountain bubbled. Vines hung from the garden walls, giving the edges a jungle-like look, but with careful searching Stephanie located Aunt Helen in a far corner. Helen appeared to be engaged in an intense debate with a large rose bloom.

Stephanie let the curtains fall back into place. No, she decided, going out there now would be a mistake.

In desperation fueled by boredom, Stephanie began milling around the library. Granny Hilda and Grandpa Drummond's library displayed three trophy heads on the walls. The north wall sported an elk head, while the east wall was graced by the presence of a javelina and a mountain lion. Granny Hilda had told her that these had once belonged to their great grandfather James, who was a civilian packer with the Army in Arizona when they pursued Geronimo. He'd personally shot the hapless animals and had their heads mounted on plaques.

They were depressing things, relics of human wastefulness, which were now moldering away. A bald spot gleamed like a halo above the glassy eyes of the despondent mountain lion. The elk seemed particularly moth-ridden. Of course, they were not exactly intruders, but it didn't take much imagination for Stephanie to believe that they might disturb Aunt Helen.

"Step one foot on the battle zone," Stephanie muttered suddenly to the lion. "Take the puzzle."

She sidled up to the big bay-window and sneaked another peek at Aunt Helen. No longer addressing the rose bush, she was moving monotonously around the garden again and had been joined on the lawn by a pair of brown grackles, arrogant birds, which were pacing, squawking, and screeching in front of Aunt Helen like silly heralds. Well, Stephanie thought, she's okay now; she's got plenty of company out there walking around with her.

"Destiny brought this puzzle to me," Stephanie said, swinging around to address the elk head in a smooth voice of cool and calm contemplation. She breezed nonchalantly around the library, swiping the sunny surfaces of occasional tables and tipping several books off the shelves. "Destiny, destiny..." she muttered.

But this cool mood didn't last; she spun around to face the snarling javelina, a large specimen of an old male with curling tusks in a roaring red mouth. Its plaque had been mounted lower on the wall than the elk but she still couldn't reach it, if she was on the floor, not even if she stretched her arm up completely and stood on her toes. She circled to the far side of the room and, standing with her tiny shoulder blades pressed against the wallpaper, she taunted the high, snarling head. "Show yourself!" she said first, looking around the room as though her adversary were hiding behind the furniture. "I see you now, enemy!" she growled at the javelina. "A costly mistake!" She narrowed her eyes. The javelina, though fixed by the taxidermist in a rage, was now looking more like it wanted no part of what would be a highly one-sided battle with an angry eight-year-old. "I summon Wormdross!" she cried, issuing a challenge to her favorite imaginary foe. She had only recently developed a passion, which was Ku-gug-oh, and she pretended she was battling for life points many times throughout the day. "Weapon? What is my weapon, you say?"

She looked around her for any weapons. She saw two heavy glass paperweights, a short mallet with a wooly cover hanging at the side of a brass gong, and, in the far corner of the room, the very best thing, a long stick. The stick was an expensive, utterly useless souvenir blackthorn cudgel purchased during Drummond and Hildegard's tour of Scotland. Due to Stephanie's quick thinking, this stick had now found its very first use. She ran over to it and grabbed it with both hands. Lifting it slowly, the tip rose above her head. The stick was extremely heavy, and she was unprepared for that, so she couldn't keep it upright long before its weight took it crashing down on the couch cushions.

"Darn," she said.

It was a struggle, but she lifted the stick again and brandished it higher. "Wormdross it is!"

With the heavy stick wobbling above her head, she skirted the coffee table in front of the couch and stopped. She spun around and scurried back to the western wall. There she flattened herself and tried to think of something better to say. Where dreams become nightmares was all she could come up with. "Where dreams become nightmares!" she cried. She prepared herself for the onslaught against the terrible furry head with its horrible snarl.

"It's time to d-d-d-dual!" she said. This last, famous invocation was what she needed to charge the javelina in an angry rush. To punish it was her fondest desire now that it had been so impudent as to stay in place during her taunts. Running across the room she took on the stuffed head, delivering several ineffective blows on its gray bristle-covered snout. After the blows, the little beady black eyes of the animal had a hateful, injured look. The look made Stephanie seethe, but she decided to career off as though she feared a counterattack.

No sooner had she run away from the head than she changed her mind and decided she ought to rush the poor stuffed head again. She came back and whacked and walloped it with a punishing series of blows and jabs. First one side and then the other the hairy pig head felt her blows rain, on its snout, its eyes, and its open jaw.

"I will summon a monster to defeat you! I have four thousand life points left!" she said.

Drat! Stephanie ducked as the shadow of a lumbering figure crossed the curtains at the French door. Aunt Helen chose that moment to walk languidly by the library door again. Her lean shadow bent over a bed of mint and tweaked a faucet handle. Then Helen stooped and pinched a dried mesquite bean between two fingers. Straightening stiffly, Helen carried the bean to the garbage can near the gate. After dropping the bean in the trash, she paced back across the lawn. Her shadow floated on the bright green grass, floated right up to the house!

Stephanie was horrified when her Aunt Helen walked up the curved brick steps to the library's French doors and opened them!

Aunt Helen wiped her feet on a mat, parted the curtains, and stepped into the library. She looked around and found her niece crouching beside the fireplace holding a walking stick vertically above her head. Ordinarily she might have been astonished, but she was thoroughly distracted by her own cares.

"Oh, hello," said Aunt Helen drearily. "Don't let me bother you. Go on with what you're doing." She closed the door and crossed the room. She stretched her skinny frame out on the couch. She was so light she barely sunk in. She began staring at the library ceiling. "Please, pretend I'm not here. Go on doing whatever you were doing before."

With Aunt Helen on the couch, lying pale and still and saying nothing, Stephanie dropped the blackthorn stick beside the brass gong and joined her aunt, dragging a small chair to a spot right beside Aunt Helen's head, which lay on a large yellow pillow, which was embroidered with pheasants. Stephanie sat on this chair primly and then scooted around a bit to see if the legs were as wobbly as they looked. They certainly were wobbly. If she could get glue later, she could probably fix the wobble, she thought.

"What's wrong, Aunt Helen, you look kind of sad and strange and lost?" asked Stephanie.

"Nothing's wrong," said Aunt Helen staring up at the ceiling. "Nothing is wrong at all."

"Well, if nothing is wrong, can I please put a teeny braid in your hair? Right here?" Stephanie asked lifting a small section of her aunt's hair near the front. Aunt Helen nodded grimly and Stephanie clapped. "Oh, goodie!" She went to work.

"Hum-de-dum-dum," said Stephanie, "This is going to turn out great."

Granny Hilda peeked in at the door (she had been at the kitchen window never once losing sight of her daughter) and her big gray eyes took in the scene at the couch.

"Stephanie," said Granny Hilda sharply to her granddaughter, "let's not worry your aunt."

"No, Mom, let her be," said Helen and Stephanie smiled a satisfied smile of superiority at her granny.

Granny Hilda hesitated, and then decided they looked peaceful enough for the moment. "I'll bring you girls a late snack. The lasagna I'm making is not cooperating."

"Okay, we'll just be here together doing stuff and playing," said Stephanie smugly.

When Grandma Hildegard had gone, Stephanie sighed and waited politely for her aunt to talk. She remembered she was not supposed to pester her aunt, but talking in a friendly fashion might not be pestering.

"It's terrible that you look so strange and sad-like."

Aunt Helen didn't say anything.

"I wasn't supposed to say that."

"That's all right," said Helen.

"This braid will help you."

"Do you think so?"

"Yes, um, I happen to know so. People with braids in their hair hardly ever look sad. Except on the cover of a book called *Misunderstood Moll*. And maybe that girl named Heidi did look sad when she was in that sleigh seeing her grandfather chase her down the mountain, you know? 'Heidi! Heidi!' and all that stuff."

"Uh huh," said Aunt Helen blandly.

"The teeny braid is finished," said Stephanie, "It's the best one I ever put in anyone's hair. It looks beautiful in yours. I wish my hair was sort of skinny and flat like yours."

"Thank you."

When the tea and cookies came (on a tray Granny Hilda set on the table with a worried look at the two of them), and they were alone again, Stephanie tried to stay quiet but eventually she broke down. "Listen, Aunt Helen. I have this terrible secret to tell you."

"What?" asked Helen blankly.

"Oh, it's been just terrible for a whole long time. I gotta tell somebody."

"Are you in love with a boy at school?" asked Aunt Helen in a disinterested monotone.

"No! Aunt Helen, that's sickening."

"Okay."

"What it is is I have been wanting something very, very much," said Stephanie. She scooted the chair around to get closer to her aunt's head.

"Hmmm?" said Aunt Helen, lost in her own thoughts.

"It's a thing. Guess. Guess what it is that I've been wanting so much," Stephanie whispered into her aunt's ear.

The guessing game went on for quite an interval, there being so many sighs and lengthy pauses on Aunt Helen's part between the half-hearted guesses like "did you want a pretty doll with a china face?" or "did you want a lot of candy?" Finally, Stephanie revealed that what she had wanted for many, many years was her very own brain.

"What do you mean?" asked Aunt Helen in horror.

Of course, what she meant by that, as she quickly explained to her confused aunt, was that she had wanted someone else's brain, or a small piece of it, possibly in its own ornate Japanese wooden box with a clever sliding lid, because someone at school had opened one of those in front of Stephanie once and she had loved that box. Yes, a box with its own brain in it would suit her. She explained to her aunt that she had been frustrated for most of her life of eight years by people not letting her have the things she wanted to have, like her own brain. Everybody was always stopping her from having things, Stephanie complained. Her parents would search her room and throw out some of the things, or forbid her to have others. Aunt Helen perked up a little at this complaint, seeing an element of her current predicament in her young niece's words, and thereafter she managed to speak in something other than a monotone and even asked her niece for more details. Stephanie provided these, and how!

She explained that she had wanted a whole bunch of things that people wouldn't let her have like her own snake—a corn snake would do if they wouldn't let her have a real rattler—and a rubber pirate sword, which didn't have to have a skull on it if it upset them so much, but it had to look real, so that she could play with Melvin Jonson sometimes, and her parents had gotten mad at her for that and talked and talked about how that was bad until they made her cry, and a book called *Horrible Ghost Tales*, and more importantly, her very own piece of a brain and she intended to get them all anyway. Today, she explained, she wanted the brain. She thought she might get a piece of brain out of one of those animal heads hanging on the walls.

Aunt Helen thought for a while about what Stephanie said.

"You know, what you just said was pretty important," said Aunt Helen, "It's important, even for adults to know what they really want. If you want that piece of brain, you should try to get it. That is the very thing you ought to do. Do it today. Do it now. Don't wait for somebody else's permission."

Stephanie explained that whenever she wanted to do anything like that—getting a brain piece—something called 'her fertile imagination' was blamed.

"I'm not going to blame that," Aunt Helen

said earnestly, "A fertile imagination is better than an infertile one."

This surprised Stephanie, who was used to opposition, and when Stephanie explained that she had picked the elk trophy to attack instead of the snarling javelina or the mountain lion because its head stuck out the farthest, Aunt Helen said it made sense, though it didn't really. Aunt Helen also explained briefly that she thought Stephanie's curiosity exceeded her knowledge of taxidermy; Aunt Helen added that Stephanie might be laboring under the false impression that the taxidermist had left a dried-up chunk of elk brain inside the elk head, but such a belief was only logical and who knew but what it was true? Stephanie asked what taxidermy was. Aunt Helen said that was not too important and Stephanie should just go ahead with what she wanted. Such notions grip you when you're eight, Aunt Helen explained. The difference was when you were older you stopped yourself from doing anything. Well, she wasn't going to stop Stephanie. Besides, everyone hated those stuffed heads.

Stephanie stood back and looked at the silly elk head.

"Here I go!" she proclaimed.

With Grandpa Drummond's blackthorn stick held level, Stephanie marched toward the elk. The poor head stared stoically ahead when Stephanie stomped to a halt beneath it and to one side, flipped the stick around, and braced the blackthorn branch against the seat of a wing chair. She used the tall stick to help her step onto the seat.

Once she was standing on the chair, Stephanie raised the stick in the air quickly. Intending to give the innocent elk a solid whack aside its head, she lost control of the long heavy stick again and watched in horror as its tip dropped and neatly harpooned a beautifully illustrated gardenia on the library's wallpaper. The rubbery tip stuck to the old paper and then ripped a crooked gash through several feet of wall covering.

"Oh, my gosh," said Aunt Helen, taking slightly more interest in the world around her as the stick ripped the enormous gash.

Next, the momentum of the falling stick catapulted Stephanie over the armrest of the wingchair. Stephanie and the stick fell with a terrible clatter and the stick struck a large blown glass vase on the table in front of Aunt Helen. The vase shattered into three pieces that shot dangerously in as many directions.

"Golly!" said Aunt Helen. With the smashing of the vase directly in front of her, Helen blinked twice and seemed to become vaguely human again. "You took quite a fall there. Are you okay? Any part of you broken?"

"No, I'm okay," said Stephanie cheerfully

from the rug. "I fall off of stuff all the time. All I broke was that dumb old green vase. I thought it looked like a big old ball of snot anyways. Did granny like it?"

"No, don't worry about it. It's just something Mom and Dad had around the house. It was Finnish or something. They have lots of stuff. Too much stuff," said Helen, sniffing. "What do you want to do now?"

"I'm not giving up on the brain," said Stephanie. "I'll just hide the broken glass." Stephanie got up from the rug quickly and gathered the pieces of the vase. She lifted a pillow at Aunt Helen's feet and placed the glass lumps in the corner of the couch. She propped the pillow back in place.

"I won't stick my feet there," said Aunt Helen, cooperatively.

Stephanie didn't reply because she was busy dragging the stick back to the chair. Once she had returned to the front of the wing chair, she placed the black branch against the chair arm, and stepped back into the seat. Slowly, she lifted the stick once more. This time, when she wielded it above her head, she moved it carefully.

Stephanie treated the elk to several head bashings, and with every whack Aunt Helen seemed to cheer up and pulled herself to a sitting position on the sofa with the tea cup and saucer in her hands. She was watching everything happily, eagerly from her position on the couch across the room. It was refreshing not knowing what was going to happen next and feeling that it might be something big and awful. A certain part of her shattered psyche felt guilty for not stopping her niece, but another part was enjoying the whole spectacle of someone doing exactly what they wanted.

BOOM! The large moldering elk head took a jarring smack on the thick side of its neck. BANG! Stephanie hit it below its large ears and under the antlers.

The violated elk head emitted a great and terrible groan.

"Oh, my goodness," said Helen, her eyebrows rising, "This is terrible," she giggled.

The groan continued, long and loud; it resonated in the room. Dust rose in puffs, a fine shower of elk hairs dropped on the rug, but nothing else happened. Then, they both noticed a stream of adobe dust sieving out from behind the trophy; it ran straight down in front of the gardenia wallpaper so thin and fast that it seemed as though the flowers were quivering. A crumbly brown pile of adobe was accumulating on the carpet against the high baseboard. "Uh-oh," Stephanie said, unable to take her eyes off the pile of dirt, yet attempting a rather ineffective and painfully slow scramble off the chair. She put her hand down in places where the chair wasn't and her legs didn't seem to know which direction they usually bent.

What followed was a lengthy, ripping noise, a tearing asunder of some terrible proportion, undetectable by the human eye, and causing no corresponding movement besides the falling dirt.

Then, suddenly, the huge head shot forward with a severe nod.

"Oh-h-h-h-h!" Stephanie gasped as she leapt back.

A cataract of adobe opened behind the stuffed elk head.

"God! This is funny! I've hated that thing for years!" said Helen.

The head kept coming forward and the wallpaper ripped. The head and the stick and Stephanie hit the floor.

"Oh my gosh!" cried Helen.

The elk head fell, bounced on the carpet, and rolled to a spot near the wall.

There the ravaged elk head lay, placidly staring at the ceiling.

"Phew!" Stephanie said, relieved that the falling head had missed her. She propped herself up on both elbows, rolled to her side and grabbed the walking stick again.

The elk head, which was near her, could not have been more detached and disinterested, though there was a certain swarthy sadness around its glass eyes. Perhaps it sensed what she was up to?

"This is terrible, just terrible," said Stephanie, standing over it and realizing what she had done.

"Oh, I wouldn't worry about it," said Aunt Helen placidly. She took another sip of tea. "Everyone hates those heads except for Dad, and I really think he doesn't like them all that much either. He just thinks they're historical. He doesn't really care about them. No brain, though?" she asked, peering around the side of the coffee table to see. The whole operation of the head being hit and ripping off the wall had revived her spirit even more than before. She talked like a normal person.

"No brain," said Stephanie standing above the head and sighing. Stephanie tried jamming the stick up a nostril and with a mighty thrust, she probed and pushed and explored, whirling the stick like the handle to a music box, and prying upwards. Nothing. "If I had scissors, I could cut its head open, but I don't know—maybe there isn't a brain in there."

"Don't you think so?" asked Aunt Helen.

"No. No brain for me."

Stephanie went to the wing chair and flopped. She sat looking sad until suddenly she cheered up a bit thinking that she would have to do something really special to the mountain lion.

"Oh, the lion now?" asked Aunt Helen, seeing Stephanie heading for it. "Yes," said Stephanie slowly. She tried to think what it could be that she could do to it that would be fun. Hitting it didn't seem to be enough. She put the blackthorn stick down. She wondered if she ought to paint it. But paint would be too hard to find. She knew she couldn't get the little cans in Granny Hilda's sliding kitchen drawers open; she had already tried. There ought to be something she could do to it that would use something in the room.

Something, something. She paced the room like a caged animal. All at once she saw a short, but sharp, letter opener stuck as a place holder in a coffee table book. She pounced upon it, yanking it out of the book happily.

"I might be able to get the glass eye out of the lion," said Stephanie.

"But would you want one of those?" asked Aunt Helen. She knew as she was saying this that she ought to be telling her niece not to damage another trophy, but she couldn't stand the idea of stopping anyone's fun.

"I wanted a brain more," Stephanie said, "but I guess it would be kinda fun to have a glass eye. Yes, a glass eye from a lion in its own little sliding box!"

Spurting over to the chair again, she began dragging it across the carpet. The chair was heavy and it took her quite a while until it was under the mountain lion head. Once it was there, she stepped into the seat again and onto the arm of the chair. She jabbed the letter opener around the stuffed head thinking about how she might be able to get at the eyes. Finally, she found a vulnerability. It seemed to her that if she sank the letter opener into the outer corner of the left eyelid, she could make a prying motion at the glass eye and with luck the thing would pop out.

Getting that glass eye out would be quite a prize! Who else had the glass eye of a stuffed lion?

She got right to work. She pried and pried.

"Come on, little old lion," coaxed Stephanie.

"Any luck?" asked Aunt Helen.

"Not yet," said Stephanie grimacing.

She kept working until she heard a ripping sound and got the result she wished for with a suddenness that astonished even her.

PLOP! The lion's glass eyeball shot out of the head in a funny, crazy way and arced across the library where it hit the big brass gong covered with Chinese words and the gong went BINK and the glass eye ricocheted off and struck a table and rolled across the carpet.

A real glass eye out of stuffed lion head!

Aunt Helen laughed and clapped. "Bravo!

Bravo!" she cried.

Gee, this was great, thought Stephanie. An eye out of a lion. And it was hers. This was going to be a wonderful day. And she had cheered Aunt Helen up.

"Now all you have to do is find it," said Aunt Helen.

Which proved easier said than done.

Aunt Helen watched her niece crawling around on the carpet until she thought of something. She placed her cup and saucer down on the coffee table and stood up. "I'm going to help," she said dramatically, and she dropped onto her knees on the library carpet. Aunt Helen hadn't crawled anywhere for a long time, maybe since she had been a little girl. Gee, she thought, as she did it, crawling was therapeutic. Stephanie crawled frantically this way and that looking for the glass eye on the rug.

"This is a great! What a good game! Aren't we really having fun?" said Aunt Helen, crawling around wildly with her niece. She did sense vaguely that her knees might be receiving some rather nasty carpet burns. "This is so much fun!"

"Aunt Helen," said Stephanie, sitting still, "crawling around on the floor isn't much of a game. How long has it been since you played anything?"

Aunt Helen sat back on her heels. "Well, I

guess it's been too long if I think this is so much fun. Am I useless?"

"You gotta play more. Hey, we've got all weekend," said Stephanie, excitedly.

"Yes, but first we have to find that eye for you," said Aunt Helen.

Wherever it had gone, that glass eye had gone there thoroughly, because they couldn't see it on the Persian carpet pattern no matter which way they crawled or how often they rested their heads down close to the carpet fibers, because glass might glint that way. Helen even strained herself trying to stick her arm as far back as possible under the couch.

"Hey, where you going?" asked Stephanie.

"I was thinking about starting a painting," said Aunt Helen, and she had a small amount of interest in her voice, "I really, really want to. And right now! I've got an idea of what I want to do for my first painting. It's come to me after all this crawling!"

Stephanie thought about Granny Hilda's words, about how she was supposed to let Helen do whatever she wanted. "Okay, then," she said, a little sadly.

When Aunt Helen was walking out of the library, Stephanie spoke under her breath to herself. "I knew you wouldn't last long playing with me."

Stephanie kept crawling and scooping her hand under the couch again and again and scooping along the carpet over the pattern. She lifted some pillows and peeked under the curtains.

Gee! She mustn't lose it. Where could it have gone?

She slouched back in front of the lion. She stood below it, looking up. How much better it would look completely shaved rather than having that bald halo; it was a shame but someone had locked Grandpa Drummond's bathroom door and she couldn't see an easy way to break the lock.

Stephanie skipped out the library door and down the carpeted hall of her grandparents' home. Frankly, she was disappointed about the lost mountain lion eye, and she vowed that after dinner, when her grandparents sent her to bed, she would stay awake and sneak out in order to continue her search of the carpet. Until then, she would find something else to play.

Making her way down the wide hall, she smacked the people in the oil paintings which had been arranged by her grandfather in a highly artistic fashion on one wall. All of the paintings featured mountain men and smoky Native American camps, because Grandpa Drummond was crazy about the lives and legends of the early mountain men, especially those in Arizona. Stephanie halted in mid skip in front of a large painting with a big lake. There was no one there to smack. "Hey," she said, "where are all the peoples? Peoples, where are you? Huh?" Stephanie frowned while searching the entire picture for the figure of a human. And then she got her wonderful idea.

She realized that it might be fun, and probably important, to add a little person of her own to the painting. Near that big flat gray rock, she could slip a funny naked boy. He would be halfway into the cold water. Hey, thought Stephanie, it was an amazing idea for a day which had been so thoroughly awful—Aunt Helen was going to be a big disappointment as a playmate. Well, what had she expected, she reminded herself; adults were unable to play anything for long. They had short attention spans when it came to playing and long attention spans when it came to correcting children and other boring stuff.

Stephanie walked into the kitchen and said 'hi' to Granny Hilda who was layering lasagna noodles at the bottom of a large glass pan. She told Stephanie the noodles kept splitting and falling apart. When Granny Hilda turned her back to deal with a slippery, ripping noodle, Stephanie quickly searched a cup in the corner of the counter for a black permanent marker she'd seen. It was there! And a pocketknife, too! She grabbed the marker, stuffed the knife in her pant pocket, and ran back to the painting in the hall.

On tiptoe, she brought the marker quickly to the spot she had chosen and she placed the small boy beside the rock, bathing in the aqua mountain water. She didn't think about how to draw him at all; she just scribbled him in. And he turned out to be cuter than she had imagined him to be!

Now that the boy she'd imagined could go swimming in the water, she stuck the cap on the marker and placed it in her pocket, then she spun around, and hastened away toward the front of the house. In a front room, near a low shelf with a lamp on it, Stephanie froze. She saw a very strange and horrible thing she had never noticed before. It floored her, actually. It was an animal skull—she didn't know what kind of animal—but it was covered with little rectangular turquoise stones, bright ones that were stuck all over it so they almost touched each other. That poor thing all stuck up like that, thought Stephanie, what a horror! And there were gems for the taking. Stephanie stooped down and found she could crawl right onto the shelf beside the skull. She pulled herself in and had plenty of room. What a safe nook she had found. No one would notice her down there, if she stayed still. If they came looking for her, she wouldn't talk.

She wormed her pocketknife out and got busy picking at the stones with the little knife.

It took a lot of prying to make the first stone pop off. Then a second came more easily because there was a space where she could get the knife blade under. It was wonderful fun making them plink off into the air, though it took some prying on the different corners of the stones to find the edge that was most likely to lift. When they did shoot off, she reached out wherever they flew and pocketed them. It took her quite a while to get enough of them, but what a lot of turquoise gems she'd gotten.

Eventually, Stephanie tired of popping stones off the skull and she sat and looked at it. She took it into her lap. Poor sad animal, thought Stephanie (not remembering the stuffed heads she had only just finished abusing) someone really ought to bury it. She would make that a job for the weekend. That poor thing deserved a break after all, someone had glued stones all over its head!

Stephanie crawled out from the cramped spot on the shelf, cradling the skull. She lifted it in front of her. "I am so sorry about you dying. That is just the terribliest thing," she said to it, "but I am going to make everything okay. I got most of those stones off you, but you really ought to be buried, you know. That would be the right thing for you." She gave it a kiss on the head. "I don't know what my grandpa was thinking keeping you unburied. Really."

Stephanie carried the skull outside to the back garden. There was no sign of Aunt Helen or anyone else, so Stephanie hid the skull under a bush. Then she came back in and turned her attention to an interesting belt displayed on the wall—with another skull! It was a baby deer head wrapped in a purple scarf with the belt hanging off the skull. The belt was hung low enough for Stephanie to touch the strange white paper-like cocoons that it was made of, row after row of cocoons, each like a little white shell with something inside to make a rattle.

Stephanie took the knife out of her pocket again, opened it, and sliced off one of the cocoons. She put the cocoon to her ear and shook it. Very nice! She cut off a lot more and filled another pocket. The deer head was mounted too high otherwise she would have taken it outside also. "I'll get a chair tomorrow," promised Stephanie to the baby deer skull, "and get you buried. Don't you worry about yourself. I'm gonna take care of you."

Next, Stephanie went to look at all those old pots which her grandpa kept on one of the low shelves in the living room. They were white pots with big red swirls that looked like nothing Stephanie could comprehend. Just then, Granny Hilda checked in on her. She seemed happy to see Stephanie looking at those pots.

"Dinner in about forty minutes," said Granny. "Where's your aunt?"

"She's painting," said Stephanie.

"Oh, she **is** is she!" exclaimed a delighted Granny Hilda, "Well, that's the best thing for her. She said she was going to paint?"

"Uh huh, that's what she said. I think I'll use one of my Egyptian pharaoh cards to defeat these pots," Stephanie explained.

"That's nice," said Granny Hilda. "As soon as your grandfather gets back, I'll tell him you were admiring his favorite Cibola pots. He'll be so happy. They are cherished old things of his." Granny Hilda smiled at Stephanie who smiled back in a simpering fashion.

The instant Granny disappeared Stephanie stacked two of the pots together and carried them outside. Several of those grackle birds, which Stephanie had seen walking with her aunt, strode across the lawn authoritatively in the cool pink twilight. In the center of the lawn the fountain bubbled loudly onto the backs of Koi fish. Stephanie placed the pair of pots on the edge of the fountain and sat on the edge herself watching the orange, white and black splotched fish for a while. It would be great to catch one of those huge things in a pot, but they kept away when she tried. She decided to fill both pots with water.

Stephanie started to think that it was very sad that no one had used those pots for anything, probably for years and years, if they were actually so old. Had the old Indian lady potter meant for them never to be used again? Did the potter lady give them to Grandpa for his collection? It didn't seem right that something so nice never got used. The lady who made them probably wouldn't have liked it if they never had a reason for being. Maybe she'd have wanted Stephanie to use them in a camping game?

The well of a mesquite tree nearby had been raked, but under a bush the yardman had left wet mesquite beans in a pile. Stephanie scooped handfuls of them and tossed them in the pots. Then she found some black bean pods on a smaller tree and she threw them in, too. It was fun filling the old pots with beans. The lady who made those would probably be happy about what Stephanie was doing, she thought.

Stephanie lifted one pot of the wet beans and placed it on her head. She stumbled around the yard, crying, "I have lost my way on the trail." She spoke in what she thought would be the sound of the raspy voice of a crabby tribal elder. "Oh! Oh! Now I return to my camp and what do I see? Where is my fire?" she cried. "You let it go out, you stupid invisible peoples! You are no good. I need a fire. Go into the forest, peoples! Every one of you, I order you," she said. "Go, I say, go! At once, away with you, little bad peoples."

She plopped the pot on the grass and assumed the part of the nervous, worthless people, who were hotfooting it around the garden in search of kindling. "We're going where you tell us to go. Don't beat us you mean old lady! Ay, ouch!" She pretended to fend off the blows of the disapproving elder.

Grandpa's gardener did a thorough job of clearing garden waste. There wasn't any kindling for Stephanie, so she snapped off the branches of some shrubs and stripped them of leaves. While she was at it, she snapped off the tops of some flowers to flavor the soup. She tossed the flower tops in the pots, and piled the stripped branches on the grass. She set the pots on the imaginary fire and knelt before them. "I am happy, my peoples," she said, in the voice of the demanding elder. "You have done goody-nesses." But now Stephanie wanted to stir the mesquite beans, and she remembered that the old garage had an amazing collection of tools in it. At Christmas she might even have seen some rusty spoons on top of a coffee can full of bolts.

Stephanie scrambled to her feet and crossed the lawn. When she was almost at the big wooden door to the garage, Granny Hilda came out of the house and began looking everywhere behind shrubs and trees and garbage cans. She seemed to be picking up leaves. Granny looked shocked when she examined those headless flowers and the shrub with all the branches broken off it. Stephanie thought she ought to hide herself, and she found that the south side of the garage was covered with a dormant Queen's Wreath vine; the stout, reddish tendrils made a dusty curtain that Stephanie could part and squeeze through. Granny came straight toward her, but luckily it turned out that her objective was to peek into the garage. The door was ajar, so Granny looked in for an instant, smiled, and backed away. Stephanie didn't feel like being seen or heard by Granny right then so she hesitated to come out; even if Granny Hilda's back were turned, the garage door always made a loud scraping sound on the concrete. Just when Stephanie was getting really tired of waiting for Granny to disappear, and Granny was getting closer to the pots with the beans and flowers in them, a timer went off in the kitchen and Hilda left the yard. Stephanie parted the dried vine and emerged. She snuck around the garage door.

The garage smelled of turpentine and linseed oil. Several lights were on like bright suns, and for an instant Stephanie couldn't see a thing. Finally, there, with her back to Stephanie, slouched her Aunt Helen on a three-legged stool. Stephanie had forgotten that the garage was where Aunt Helen kept her painting supplies. Aunt Helen's apartment didn't have any place big enough to set up the kind of large paintings she was planning.

Aunt Helen was drooping before an enormous blank canvas. At first Stephanie thought her aunt was sitting motionless, but then Stephanie noticed that she made a slight movement, a rubbing motion of a soft rag over the hairs of a paintbrush, and after she rubbed it, she would reach out and dip it in a glass jar and bring it back to slowly daub it on the rag. Her posture showed defeat. Her back curled over toward the big blank canvas as though she were confronting an angry white animal. Even when a few dried leaves from the vine scuttled through the open door and danced around behind Stephanie, Aunt Helen didn't turn around.

Then Aunt Helen groaned, long and low, a groan of utter despair. Finally, she spoke. "I had the idea. I knew what I was doing. I had a way in my mind to paint modern clouds above a modern city."

"But you can't paint clouds, Aunt Helen," Stephanie chirped. Aunt Helen spun around.

"Oh, it's you. Are you telling me I can't paint?" said Aunt Helen despondently.

Stephanie stepped into the garage. "You can't paint clouds, because they're too high up. You could never get up to them with a ladder made by the best ladder maker in the world." Stephanie looked at her aunt with a face that attested to her sincere effort to educate.

Aunt Helen smiled weakly and laid her paintbrush on the ledge of the easel. The canvas had been prepared meticulously; it had been stretched and coated thoroughly with rabbit glue, which she thought superior to gesso, and she had made sketches of what she wanted to paint, but what she had been actually doing day in and day out until now was puzzling over gross domestic product and exchange rates. Up until that day, she had been living one of those modern lives of quiet despair, which the man who camped at the pond criticized so astutely a hundred and forty years ago.

Why the sadness she felt for a year hadn't prompted her to make the leap to painting earlier was complicated. She entertained doubts about her talent in art, and those doubts destroyed her enjoyment. You could even say she was harassed by demons, inner critics, and couldn't face selling her art to anyone, or, more extremely, even doing her art, as long as those demons told her that her unmade art wasn't going to be good enough.

She often wondered how it could be that she would place a single daub of paint on a canvas and immediately have doubts about every possible thing about the daub, its location on the canvas, the intensity of the hue, the brush used, and even the amount of linseed oil and turpentine in the mix.

And these clouds Helen aspired to paint were rather nebulous things; they would appear in her first series of ideal paintings, which she hadn't yet painted, above deteriorated cities, haciendas, mysterious jungles, or high desert mountains. An oak tree on a grassy plain might have an interesting cloud above it in her ideal paintings, or a crowded city skyline might reveal a single, enigmatic blotch of white. That was what she had in mind. She wanted to depict all kinds of modernist clouds: cumulonimbus clouds with wispy trailing edges, banks of grimy fog, billowing storm clouds with iron-colored edges, or extraordinary pink clouds at dawn, etc., and every day she itched to get started on this broad canvas in her parents' garage, but still it awaited her first brushstroke.

"I ought to go inside," she said in despair. She put the rag beside the brush. "I thought after I was in the library with you and we talked about what people wanted to do–about you wanting to get that piece of elk brain and then the glass eye–I thought I ought to try to paint. But I don't think I'm quite ready yet. A part of me is holding me back. Maybe it's the critic or something." Aunt Helen stood up. "I wanted to paint the essence of clouds, actually, not their physical attributes, but their essential nature, the fogginess, the spirit of them in the sky. I wanted to capture their airy nebulousness, and the way they change and flow over the face of the earth. So, you see, it was more complicated than real clouds that you really see in the sky. I was thinking about the clouds you feel."

"Oh, well," Stephanie replied, "okay. I think you ought to just do that, what you just said, instead of sitting there the next time you decide to paint, okay? Anyway, are you going to stay overnight?" asked Stephanie when Aunt Helen turned off the garage lights, led Stephanie outside, and swung the big wooden door closed behind them.

"I suppose they'll make me," said Aunt Helen. "Uncle Will is working until late Sunday and Granny thinks I need company tonight." Uncle Will was Aunt Helen's husband and at times he stayed days at the missile plant.

"You might not be able to sleep. In a strange house like this," Stephanie suggested. "Grandpa has a lot of horrible stuff all over the place."

"I suppose I might have trouble sleeping,"

Aunt Helen agreed.

"Then I know what will help you. I'm going to read you a bedtime story before you go to sleep! Grandpa Drummond has some really great books in his library. I found one last Christmas that was so interesting. We could act it out."

"That sounds nice."

"After dinner, when I get ready for bed, you meet me up there in the second story where my bedroom is and I'll get you all relaxed, okay!"

Aunt Helen promised to do just that.

When Stephanie put her hand on the doorknob to the library and prepared to enter it for a second time that Friday evening, several hours had passed since she had essentially destroyed the room.

During the family dinner, Grandpa Drummond had called her 'his little snickerdoodle' and chucked her chin. And right after dinner he had fed her ice cream, but none of that made Stephanie forget that she had promised to get a bedtime book for Aunt Helen from Grandpa Drummond's library.

She was almost afraid to go back inside after the mess she knew she had made. When the door swung open, she saw the room was dark, and in the murky light emanating from the early moon, Stephanie noticed that some of the edges of the windowpanes outside were thick with dirt and messy spider webs. She crept across the carpet keeping an eye out for the lion's glass eye; she sure wished she had gotten that thing after all the trouble she'd gone through.

There was the hole in the wall where the elk head had fallen and a pile of dirt on the carpet near the baseboard. The grim elk head stared fixedly at the dark ceiling. Stephanie glanced at the lion. Without the lights on, you could barely see that it was missing an eye. Stephanie felt nervous and guilty. The room was creepy enough without having the damaged heads despising her.

During the prior Christmas, as she had mentioned to Aunt Helen, Stephanie had made an eager search through her grandparents' bookshelves. In one far corner of the room, where she headed now, she remembered, one shelf which looked as though a team of bobcats had been brought in and set to the task of shredding the covers of black and red velvet annuals and albums. The old tomes with titles like *Benson Beauties* and *Copper State Capers* promised hours of harmless escapades, if you could get past the spidery strings tickling your forearms and calves. There were foxy and dog-eared war documents from the files of old Fort Critterdon stripped naked of their covers (what depredations they had endured!) and stacks of broken and beaten book covers which had collapsed without their pages. And on one momentous afternoon she found a book which was wonderful. It concerned a murder! She would get that book to read to Aunt Helen.

And it was there still on the same shelf. *Blood on the Apache Moon: Terror Tales of Olde Arizona*. That was the medicine for her aunt before bed. That would be bound to do her a great deal of good.

As she left the library with the wonderful terror tales book tucked under her arm, she got an image in her mind of a certain funny mask with all sorts of hair on it, a long, black, scraggly beard and a huge nose. It was some weird Mexican thing that Grandpa never noticed, and she had touched the wiry beard once. She would like to see how that hair was attached. Or, more truthfully, she would like to pull some of that hair out by clumps and throw the handfuls into the fountain with the big goldfish swimming in it. A glob of beard hair floating on the pond surface would be really funny if somebody thought it was an animal and maybe some of the fish would bite the hair and she could yank them out of the water tomorrow. She would like to get a hold of one of those incredibly fat goldfishes.

But she thought of something that was even better. Something that almost made her shiver it was so amazing.

If she wore the mask, it might surprise Aunt Helen right before the terror tales!

She found the mask on a narrow table in the living room. She snatched it off the table and put it on.

Down the hall toward the staircase, Stephanie crept with the mask on her face. Boy, this would give Aunt Helen a jolt that would bring her into reality, if nothing else did, and afterwards she would be able to paint her modern cloud paintings.

As she put her foot on the bottom stair, another funny idea popped into her head. She recalled where she had stashed Grandpa Drummond's razor. Right before dinner, when she came in with Aunt Helen, she had discovered Grandpa Drummond had left his bathroom door ajar. It was easy to get the shaver, but she hadn't had time to shave the lion before dinner was announced. She had dropped the electric razor into that big basket in the library and it was still there. This mask face needed to see a barber.

Stephanie ran back into the dark, scary library. With the mask on, it was a little difficult to see into the bottom of the large basket, but she finally felt around until she touched the shaver. She could see herself buzzing the shaver over the mask beard and maybe the lion's chin.

Stephanie switched the shaver on. It buzzed loudly and vibrated in her hand.

But who was coming?

Just before the footsteps reached the library, Stephanie switched off the razor and found she could hide behind the enormous basket. She still had the mask on her face.

Grandpa Drummond lumbered down the hall of his home. His long white beard and shoulder length white hair was authentic for his mountain man parade the next day, and his gray eyebrows twisted in contortions as difficult to follow as a child's first attempt at cursive writing. Drummond stood erect, but big bellied, had shiny pink cheeks, and a large red nose. He had been heading for the kitchen, but he came into his library after hearing a bee buzzing in the bay window. He'd heard them trapped there before; he was sensitive about trapped bees, but on his way to the window he switched on a small table lamp and was very surprised to see some of his books tilting out of the bookshelves or, even worse, lying on the floor with their backs cruelly strained. As surprised as he was by the books, he gasped to see the stuffed elk head on the floor, a rip in the wallpaper, and a giant hole in his adobe wall where the head had been. Drummond went to inspect the hole and the rip, when a strange hairy form in a shadowy corner seemed to leap up from behind the big basket, and when he spun around to see what it was, and cried "Who's there!", one foot stomped the carpet, or what he supposed was going to be the carpet. Instead, his foot met something else. This something else provided about as much traction as you would imagine a round glass orb would.

Grandpa Drummond's foot slipped, he floundered, and his left leg shot forward. His hip collapsed downward, and he fell with a tremendous crashing boom. For a moment, he lay there in shock and confusion and then a small wail of misery arose.

"Hilda!" he shouted after the wail.

From behind the basket, Stephanie gasped and covered her mouth.

Grandpa Drummond waited.

"Hilda!"

His gaze traveled around the room and he stared down at the fallen elk head, and up at the battered javelina and the mountain lion, which seemed to be winking at him. No doubt he was hallucinating from the fall, hitting the ground so hard. But he could swear that lion had something wrong with its expression, something different...

He pulled himself across the library carpet toward the couch. When he reached the couch, his hand ran forward under the sofa pillow, but shot back right away. "Glass?" He threw the pillow back. "Hilda!"

"What? What have you done?" Hilda's voice could be heard coming down the hall. Upon entering the library and finding her husband sprawled on the carpet, she exclaimed: "Oh, Drummond!"

"I slipped on something and fell." Grandpa Drummond said this in a distracted voice as he made sure that his hand hadn't been cut by the broken glass. "Do we have a new maid service?"

"Yes, yes, we do. But oh, my goodness. What have you done? Oh, dear." She crossed the room and dropped to the side of her injured husband. Before she got to him, she wiped her hands on a tea towel and tossed it on the couch. "What have you hurt?"

"Oh, nothing really. Only my pride. I need help getting upstairs. I...think...I'll be okay if I can rest my hip for an hour in bed."

"Well, that's what we'll do then. Do you think you can get to our room?"

"Yes," he said, his gaze traveled to the wall behind her and the assortment of heads. "Oh, and I almost forgot, the elk head, Hilda. It's come down. Look at the size of that hole!"

Hilda swung around. "My goodness. What's happened? We'll have to get Dr. Adobe in here again."

And when his wife turned toward him, he bobbed his head around hers to keep his gaze focused on the stuffed lion head. "I found the elk head down and these pieces of broken glass hidden under this pillow. Wasn't that the Swedish vase, the Gertrick Von Frick, which you got from your sister?"

"Yes, I'll buy another."

"She died! All her work is very valuable. She isn't blowing anymore glass for anyone. And so many books on the floor. What could have happened?"

"I don't know. It's terrible. But whatever made you fall? Are you faint at all? Maybe too much sun out in the yard? Perhaps we should call your heart specialist?"

"No, nothing like that," said Drummond. "I thought something jumped up, but there was nothing and then I could have sworn I felt something...something underfoot. I...I think it was a small glass ball. I must have dropped a marble in here the last time I played Chinese checkers with Will. Be careful, there might be others."

Hilda helped Drummond to his feet and they slowly made their way across the room. "I don't think so, dear," she said, "The maids have vacuumed thoroughly since you last played Chinese checkers."

"And doesn't the mountain lion look funny? It seems to be winking? What's his eye doing?" Drummond thought his own eyes were playing tricks; he squinted and turned his head back toward the lion when they stood in the threshold ready to leave.

"The lion?" asked Hilda.

"Does the mountain lion...does it seem to be winking?" He stared at the stuffed head on the wall as though he had never properly seen it before. He frowned and concentrated.

"Why, no dear. It's dark in here. It doesn't," said Hilda giving it a cursory glance.

"Does that lion's eye seem to be winking? I think there's something funny about...something...it didn't look like that yesterday."

"Well dear. If you're going to let it upset you, I'll take a look at it." Hilda left Drummond hanging onto the threshold as she approached the lion head and squinted at it as it squinted back at her. "Now that you mention it, I think, one of its eyes...why, yes, it's gone! One of its eyes is missing. I don't wonder. The old thing. They're all just falling to pieces. Rotten old moldy things. They're attracting bugs into the house and they're dropping apart. All their hair is shedding. I suppose the crash of elk head falling loosened the lion's eye. It must have happened that way.

Then you stepped on it."

"I suppose. That makes sense," said Drummond. "The eye wasn't missing yesterday."

"Oh, and Drummond! You're going to be so happy!" Hilda came back to him and supported her husband as he limped toward the stairs. "While you were gone the most wonderful thing happened. Stephanie showed an interest in your special Native American things. She was studying and studying those old pots of yours like nothing you've ever seen. She was standing in front of them and just staring at them so patiently. My goodness, it was awfully cute, but, you know, it impressed me," said Hilda with a thrilled expression on her face. The fact that Stephanie picked up two of those valuable pots and took them outside to play camp with after Hilda left and the fact that they were sitting precariously on a pile of sticks on the lawn and were full of dirty water and mesquite beans was unknown to Granny Hilda. "Maybe she'll grow up to be an archeologist or an anthropologist someday," said Granny Hilda.

"An archeologist or an anthropologist?" Drummond said. "Wouldn't that be something? Do you really think she might be that interested in my collection?"

"Interested? I'm telling you, fascinated might be more like it. Yes, yes, she was just studying and studying those pots. She showed so much interest in them. Just intense. And several other things on the walls and the shelves, too."

"Well, well. This surprises me. So, you actually think you have seen her studying some of my pots...and it makes you think—this is so wonderful—that she will someday want to be working as an archeologist or, or in a museum?" Drummond hobbled beside his wife up the stairs and through the hall, past cabinets and curio-jammed shelves, toward their large bedroom that occupied a corner of the second story of their home. He began to spread his happiness thickly: "By golly! I knew she would. This is really something. A child prodigy." Reaching the threshold of their bedroom, he began to speculate along those lines. "That a child would see the beauty in a Native American pot—I won't be surprised at all if Stephanie...where is that little Stephanie of mine?" asked Drummond, pulling himself upright. "I wouldn't be surprised at all if Stephanie grows up to be a museum curator."

"Oh dear, I certainly hope so. None of my people were anything special."

Drummond let out a large groan when he eased himself onto the bed.

While Granny Hilda helped Drummond leave the library after his fall, her body blocked Drummond's view of Stephanie who scampered out from behind the large basket where she had been hiding. She slipped out the doorway behind her grandparents in a very ingenious and happy fashion like a slithery spy, a role which Stephanie assigned herself whenever she escaped in a close call, which that certainly had been. Grandpa Drummond had nearly caught her that time, but she had proved more resourceful. She could fit behind baskets. She could sit in a room and not make a bit of noise while grownups talked.

And she could sneak up on her resting aunt. Stephanie, still wearing the hideous mask, crept up the stairs behind her grandparents and scampered toward the bedroom, the room next to Stephanie's, where her aunt was supposed to sleep. Stephanie pressed the door to Helen's bedroom open and slithered close to Aunt Helen, who was waiting for her niece.

Helen was talking to herself while she rested on the comforter cover. "I know I did the right thing by dropping out of school," she said, "but I can't feel happy about the painting yet. What is it? What am I missing? Something seems so wrong about it. I can't get myself happy."

"Auntie Helen? Oh, auntie? Oh, my aauunnnttieeee," whispered Stephanie.

Helen didn't acknowledge her niece, instead she switched from talking aloud to thinking about the terrible times she had been having in her first year in graduate school. She felt relief that she did not have to worry about passing her comprehensive exams later in the summer (that would have ruined the next six months) and she knew in a day or two she would have to contact the two other women she had befriended and planned to study with that summer. It was going to be hard to tell them she had already dropped out of the program, but she didn't regret what she had done.

"Auntie Heeellennnn," said a voice.

Helen roused herself slowly and turned her head toward the sound of her name being called.

Helen blinked.

A mass of stringy black hair with empty eye sockets, flat red skin and a horrid nose rose up slowly at the side of the bed.

"Holy shit!" she yelled, sitting bolt upright in a split second.

"Hey, don't worry, it's me!" said Stephanie pushing the mask back on the top of her head. "Hey, you said the s word."

Helen collapsed sideways—only a little—but, Stephanie thought it was an awfully wonderful sign, along with the loud yell, almost a scream. It was a wake-up yell. The kind of yell that Stephanie felt would do Helen good.

"Oh, my God," said Helen, pushing on her chest, "Oh, shit."

"You said the s word again," said Stephanie.

"Sorry, but you really scared me," said Helen.

"Don't be sorry. I sayed it a lot. Were you thinking about dropping out of school in eekie-something and all that? I want to tell you all about me dropping out, too."

"Why did you do that?" asked Helen.

"I thought it would do you some good. I think it did!" said Stephanie brightly.

While Helen recovered from her fright,

Stephanie told her aunt all about how awful her new school was and how she hadn't been awarded a green sticker, even once.

Stephanie had gotten out the bedtime book, by the time Grandpa Drummond wandered back along the hall outside the room where Helen would be sleeping.

"I hope my ankle and hip will feel stronger tomorrow," said Drummond, frowning at his foot and rotating his ankle. "I don't want to be limping in the parade." He stood in the lighted doorway and squinted at Helen and Stephanie. Stephanie quickly jammed *Terror Tales* under the bed covers.

"I'll be so disappointed if I'm not fit to march in the Mountain Man Rendezvous and Vaqueros y Hombres de Montana Parade with my little granddaughter," he said loudly from the hall. "Is that my littliest, ittliest snickerdoodliest girl in there with her auntie getting all ready for beddie-by?"

"Ah yeah," said Stephanie, raising her hand. "Right here."

"Are you going to be ready for the Vaqueros y Hombres de Montana Parade tomorrow?"

"Okay, sure," said Stephanie.

"Maybe a parade is what I need. I'll be going too," said Helen.

"O-O-O kay," said Drummond wandering off. "My little daughter and my granddaughter, my little Native American curator granddaughter, is going to be ready!"

"Whackeros?" Stephanie exclaimed from her pillow beside Aunt Helen when Grandpa Drummond had left the doorway. "Aunt Helen, you gotta tell me, do they actually have a parade of whackeros?"

"Hehe," said Helen, tittering. "You know, that's a little bit funny the way you say things." She brightened up at the prospect. "Whackero, that's very funny."

"Well, do they? Do they?"

"Yes, yes, they do, Stephanie. Each year they have a whackero parade and your grandfather is in it. Tomorrow when we wake up we have to dress like mountain men and drive to the mountains together and we'll all be in a parade of mountain men and whackeros."

"This is so weird," said Stephanie. "I mean it's just freaky!"

"Kind of."

"Are you ready for the bedtime tale, before you have to go to sleep?"

"Sure," said Aunt Helen bravely.

"Okay." Stephanie pulled the book out from under the covers. She propped it in front of her, resting the back against her bent knees. "It seems that there was a town called Bust Guts, Arizona and this tale is from that town, okay?"

"Go ahead. I hope it puts me to sleep,

though," said Helen. She shut her eyes. "I'm going to imagine all this wonderful stuff as you read it. Hope it's a really good story."

Stephanie looked for the page where she planned to begin reading. "Sure is. Um, this tale I'm gonna read you is all about this undead dead guy and it begins with the terrible and horrible part with a bloody stagecoach—it's dripping blood—and that bloody stagecoach comes a creaking and a groaning down this windy street, a dark old street in a spooky western town, and this coach is a creaking and a groaning in the spookiest, terribliest, horriblest way..."

"Did you say we're going to act this out?" asked Helen apprehensively.

The next morning, on the way to the Vaqueros y Hombres de Montana Parade in Skeleton Ridge, Arizona, a wolf's face made into a cap flopped atop Grandpa Drummond's head. It rode along in the SUV with its eyeless sockets, which were long slits that turned up at the corners, peeking over the snowy field of Drummond's shoulder-length white hair, while its folded ears waited patiently for the rustle of a rabbit to perk them up. The broad, gray-tipped tail which had been sewn freakishly to the back of the face, swished to and fro whenever Grandpa Drummond checked his mirrors, and the flattened grin on the wolf face made it seem to delight in the drive through town and Grandpa Drummond's conversation with his daughter and granddaughter.

Drummond accelerated onto the highway. He squinted at the bumper-to-bumper Saturday traffic that was heading places from the suburban two-story ranch-style homes that had recently crowded a floodplain between the edge of the city and the backside of the mountains to the north. What would they think, those preoccupied drivers, if they happened to glance out their side windows and saw in the car beside them a large bearded man, decked out in fringed deerskin, his suit of suede decorated like a Pawnee Indian? Would they imagine he was a kook? Or, with the Skeleton Ridge parade less than two hours away, would some of them recognize a mountain man when they saw him?

Drummond surveyed the purple desert mountains they motored past and felt another surge of pride at his appearance. He looked forward to the parade and was happy with the effect of the new wolf pelt and his authentic-looking deerskin coat, which he had labored over since July. The addition of some patches of embroidery and paraphernalia on his belt had improved his outfit. But all his plans of impressing his family with the spectacle of the parade had been spoilt. Drummond had not wondered aloud why his daughter and son-in-law had flown all the way to Mazatlán when he had been planning to take them to the parade, but he had certainly wanted to. Of course, he had shown the whole costume to them before they left, but nothing could match the satisfaction he would have felt if all his family had been there standing at the curb to see him. His compensation was that Stephanie, who had been left behind from the Mazatlán trip, could be in the parade with him and Helen, too, wearing a modification of his prior year's costume.

"Are you ready to be in a parade, my little Stephanie?" asked Grandpa Drummond, chucking his granddaughter's chin as she sat in the front passenger seat. "I'm so excited to take both you girls with me," he said, glancing in the rear-view mirror at Helen who sat in the back seat in her suede fringed outfit. "You do look authentic! A real frontier character," he said with pride.

"With a lot of safety pins," added Helen. Her expression was less sour than the day before, and the distracted, vacant look was gone. Strangely enough, she had slept well the night before, after Stephanie had read her that gory terror tale about the bloody stagecoach. She had also liked what Stephanie said about her doing the things she talked about, painting, when she painted and not sitting in front of the canvas worrying. It was great advice if she could just keep that simple idea in her head.

"This piece of buffalo on my back is hot!" said Stephanie, throwing a small, strapped piece of buffalo fur that granny had given her on the floor in front of her. "Where's the part where its head was? I can't even see that part. What good is this thing?"

"Are you going to like this parade, little Stephanie?" Drummond asked, ignoring her complaints and leaning toward her. "Am I going to see my littliest, ittliest snickerdoodliest girl being a star of the parade? You'd like that wouldn't you, Stephanie?"

Stephanie's eyes opened wide. "Yeah, sure." She was surprised that Grandpa Drummond wanted her to be a star of the parade. She would have to think of some exciting things to do in order to be considered a star.

Grandpa Drummond exited the freeway and headed their car to the little town at the base of Skeleton Mountain. They were beginning to climb into the gray mountains. Scrub oaks appeared on the hillsides and large cottonwoods in the dry washes.

What Grandpa Drummond talked about then was how much he liked the mountain man group, with the exception of a certain gentleman.

"Now, girls, as much as I like being in this club there's a situation that I want to warn you about before we get to the parade," said

Drummond. "There's an elderly gentleman who's in the group and he's a real pain. I mean he's an absolute jerk. This guy's such an incredible grouch! His name is Mr. Thom. We're bound to run into him, because he's never missed an outing yet. Unfortunately."

"Okay," said Stephanie.

"I'm sure you aren't going to like the man," continued her grandfather, "because he takes the fun out of the club. He's too serious, and he's obsessed with details. He's a stickler for authenticity. He doesn't want any kids in the parades and no women. Really the man is a kook, a cootie-ridden curmudgeon," said Drummond, getting more worked up. "If there is a way to ruin an activity, he finds it."

Other members of the mountain men club, Grandpa Drummond explained as they crossed a bridge, had invited women and children to dress up and march with them, dressing up in buckskins, that is, not worrying about cotton skirts and girly things. Knowing that it wasn't too authentic to have them along, Drummond said, Mr. Thom was bound to make them feel uncomfortable. In fact, Grandpa Drummond said Mr. Thom made everyone feel uncomfortable at almost every meeting.

"Oh no," said Helen, looking sadly out the window at the passing saguaros. She didn't want to have to deal with an unpleasant person when she was feeling so vulnerable.

"Well, I'll get rid of him," promised Grandpa Drummond, "but you let me handle him, okay?"

"Sure," said Stephanie brightly.

Grandpa Drummond explained that they would know Mr. Thom by his hooded black eyes that seemed to hate everyone they saw, a red face, and large ears. They would have to be careful to watch out for him, even avoid him, if possible, though the damned man always seemed to find Drummond.

Stephanie took note of all this. It was clear that besides being the star of the parade, and cheering up her aunt, she had another assignment, which was to look out for a red-faced, evil-eyed, large-eared gentleman. And bug him.

O nce in the mountain town of Skeleton Ridge, they came upon sprawling streets with a long row of antique stores on the main drag and a couple of fire engines attracting a crowd. The crowd also milled about the parade staging grounds, the tall, adobe schoolhouse, from the 1880's, where the Vaqueros y Hombres de Montana Parade was scheduled to start. A mass of people in crazy costumes (tooting band instruments, twirling batons, and leading sleepy-eyed burros) shuffled around oxen, stagecoaches, and small, unstable floats. The Chamber of Commerce, dressed like they would have been a century earlier, kept hopping on and off their float, and Apache women in early costumes sat on another float. One of the Apache women held a baby in Mutant Ninja outfit and they both watched an

I-phone.

The colors of the band uniforms, especially the gold epaulettes, shone in the early morning sun. Shadows spread across the main street. Carriages creaked. Men straightened their string ties. Ladies twirled their pink lacy parasols. Small girls and boys ran about screaming unintelligible things involving horses and mud. Everywhere the harnesses smelled of fresh coats of wax and the saddles gleamed in the sun. There were fancy dress groups in shimmering satin outfits and scruffy imitation miners talking on cell phones. A band in white shirts, denim, and kerchiefs surrounded a square-dance group that drank coffee.

Stephanie, Aunt Helen and Grandpa Drummond blundered their way through the crowd until they found the mountain man club: sixteen men all of them swathed from head-to-toe in suede. They were pretending to have an authentic Rendezvous, but they mostly milled around and shared made-up tall tales, did some mock tomahawk throwing, and pretended to drink out of jugs. They didn't impress the small-town crowd; someone sitting on the school fence shouted: "Look out for the Bed-Bug Brigade!" One fellow of the assembled crowd of mountain men walked around and his suede pants were so loose it looked like he wore diapers. Another mountain man had filmy eyes, desert eyes that had seen far too much sun and had been bleached out to a pale blue color, indistinct, but happy and full of so much light that there was no room for the original color. There were slack-jawed and confused looking old men whose beaded Ute costumes swept around behind them. Entire buffaloes seemed to have landed on their backs. Another young man had a horned buffalo headdress on and he walked with a wallowing command. He held his phone tight against his ear and kept asking, "What's the word from the parade marshal? How many minutes left? What's our ETD? Does anybody know the ETD?"

Drummond stood with his long, thoroughly fringed legs spread wide and his arms crossed over his chest. A curtain of suede fringe hung off him and the narrow fringe cuts swayed as he moved, jiggled playfully under his arms and across his chest and down his legs. Mountain man pride coursed through him. The wolf pelt on his head followed along with antics of its own, tilting and bobbing and seeming to grin at Drummond's club members.

Soon after they joined the mountain man group, Stephanie found Mr. Thom and attached herself to him.

"Are you really a cootie-ridden guy?" Stephanie asked Mr. Thom while balancing on a curb. She stood on one leg and then when

Mr. Thom tried to adjust his position so he wouldn't see her, she moved so that she stood right in front of him. She used an ingratiating, grating voice that came out of the silence around Mr. Thom like a tocsin. "Are you really a cootie-ridden curmudgeon?"

"Oh, God," whispered Helen to her father, "Is that Stephanie with the Thom character you talked about?"

Mr. Thom assessed Stephanie, the thatch of messy brown hair and the bucktooth protruding from the middle of a pinched, wan face, which was looking up at him coldly. Every element of Mr. Thom's outfit had been carefully researched; he despised children dressed up as mountain men, especially girl children. There had never been any children mountain men. The whole idea was absurd. And as far as women mountain people, he scoffed at the idea.

"No, no, ha, ha!" laughed Drummond, coming up quickly. "Who taught you those very funny words, Stephanie? She has such an advanced vocabulary for an eight-year-old, doesn't she?"

Stephanie walked away without responding to her grandfather, and Aunt Helen, Grandpa Drummond and the irritated Mr. Thom watched as she scuffed around the street, climbing curbs and twirling around, all the while rearranging the strap of the buffalo robe numerous times, shifting it from one arm to another, trying to attach it to her legs, to her chest and finally stacking the thick brown rug on one shoulder so that she resembled a teeny, hairy Quasimodo. Stephanie scampered up to Mr. Thom again.

"Mr. Thom, are you a curmudgeon?" she demanded. Stephanie stood in a commanding, but hunchbacked, stance near Mr. Thom waiting for his answer. Mr. Thom chose to ignore her.

"I said, are you a curmudgeon, mister?" Stephanie repeated, smacking his arm.

Helen had to turn away. She began snickering uncontrollably.

Drummond smiled at his granddaughter, tousled her hair, and laughed in the direction of the severe Mr. Thom, "I don't understand why I didn't get one of those little granddaughters who like ballet and chocolate candies."

Stephanie turned herself around several times, slowly.

Mr. Thom's mouth stretched into a sick smirk and he tried to stroll away.

"Curmudgeon, stop!" said Stephanie, running after him and pounding on Mr. Thom's thighs. "What's a curmudgeon?" she asked. She squinted at Mr. Thom as though she could see his curmudgeoness or his cooties better that way. When Mr. Thom leveled a cold glare at Drummond, he shrugged and smiled blankly.

Changing tacks, Stephanie commented in a proud manner: "I'm wearing a 'thentic outfit. Aren't I, Grandpa Drummond?" She spread her hands and rubbed them down the front of her costume. "All 'thentic."

Mr. Thom coldly regarded the costume her granny had so hurriedly assembled for her.

"What is a 'thentic outfit, Mr. Thom? Can you tell me if 'thentic is a tribe from round about here in old Arizonay somewheres?" She gestured cutely with her empty hands held up. She tried that cute gesture again to no effect. Getting no response from him, she made several violent kicking moves, which seemed to be karate or Tae Kwon Do or a seizure. She executed these moves while standing on one leg.

"If you keep that up you might give yourself an asthma attack," said Mr. Thom hopefully. "One of my grandnephews gives himself those all the time when he misbehaves." Mr. Thom seemed to derive a strange pleasure from remembering these attacks his grandnephew suffered.

On cue, Stephanie succumbed to a severe asthma attack, wheezing and pulling her shoulders toward her ears. She scooped her chest inward and crouched over her bony knees like some emaciated, tubercular monkey. Her weak and inconsistent breath drew itself through the large gap between her teeth and made a whistling attempt to escape, but was drawn back in instantly. She writhed and twisted artfully.

Aunt Helen became hysterically amused by her niece and had to step away.

"Are you all right?" asked an alarmed mountain man.

Mr. Thom stared at Stephanie, grunted and strolled away to the other side of the street where the phony miner was still talking on a cell phone to his wife.

Stephanie followed him happily. "Are you going someplace without me?" she asked innocently.

Mr. Thom cleared his throat. "Possibly to hell," he mumbled in the softest voice he could summon.

"What was that you said, Mr. Thom?" Stephanie waited for an answer in vain, then she started up the conversation again. "You'll be a mountain man, Mr. Thom, and I'll be the mountain girl! Aunt Helen is going to be the mountain skinny lady," Stephanie said, full of joy at the prospect. She clapped her hands together. One of her index fingers flew up a nostril and she probed around the inside.

Mr. Thom groaned.

"Were there ever mountain girls, Mr. Thom?" she asked, stopping beside him again and asking in a whiney squeal with the palms of her hands pressed together as though she were praying for Mr. Thom to tell her it was so.

"Shut up," said the old man to a small cloud in the sky.

"Shut up isn't a very nice way to talk to people," said Stephanie. "If I said that at my school in the Seahorse Room I might get in trouble with Mrs. Bowden. I might even miss recess and have to write all the numbers from one to one hundred." Then in a sing-song voice with her head tilting back and forth she added, "Or I might get 'think time!'"

Mr. Thom smiled faintly. "Please, please, little girl, why don't you give me some think time," pled the horrid Mr. Thom.

This request received her regard for several moments. "No," she figured finally, "I don't think so. Hey, do I get a gun in this parade?"

"Shut up."

"There are those words again, Mr. Thom! I think you're saying them deliberate. Why do you wear a purse, Mr. Thom?"

The old man ignored her.

"Are you a girl? 'Cause you're wearing a little purse." She pointed at it and then reached out and petted Mr. Thom's pouch. "I think it's kinda cute. Lemme pet it, will ya?"

Marching beside Helen, her grandfather, and the other mountain men, Stephanie didn't do anything bad for the first handful of blocks of the parade. Of this feat, she was justifiably proud. During that whole time, she was content to pass the admiring crowds and notice the interesting effect she had on them, for several adults and many children pointed to the small mountain girl among the group of mountain men and she felt wildly satisfied by their attention. She tried to hold herself erect and swagger a bit like the rest of the group. She wished he had a rifle like the others or some traps; those beaver traps would be just right slung on her shoulder, jingling and clanking away.

"Chaining up the beavers! We're chaining up the beavers!" Stephanie cried in every direction. Aunt Helen thought she was terribly funny, that she had never seen anything funnier, but Mr. Thom accidentally conked the side of Stephanie's head with his elbow.

Why, Stephanie grumbled, they hadn't even given her a sharp stick to carry. She would have liked a sharp stick very much indeed. What kind of mountain man was she without even a sharp stick to defend her against rabid beavers? What if she encountered a wolf pack or something? Wouldn't a real mountain man girl have a weapon to defend herself with? A measly slingshot even? Or a wonderful gun that she could use to shoot whatever challenged her. She liked to think of animals challenging her and she would whip out her gun and blast them.

Things about this parade were getting her down, especially the lack of a sharp stick. She was starting to feel sorry for herself.

But then she saw the big, green steaming pile of something lying in the street ahead. She realized pretty quickly that it might be horse pooh. She approached the pile fearfully, not exactly certain what it could be. She was not well informed about horse pooh. However, it proved to be quite fascinating stuff. It was strange to look at. She bent down to examine it and then got a whiff of the gassy stink wafting up. She quickly pinched her nostrils together and scampered away as fast as she could, hoping that the smell wasn't following. Unfortunately, a horse-faced boy with slanted green eyes liked what she did and laughed. "Look at the funny girl! She was looking at the horse poop! Look! Look!" he screamed to his brothers. That boy's laugh was contagious and soon all his brother, and lots of other people, were laughing at what she did.

The mountain men, especially Mr. Thom, marched on, impervious to the effect the little girl was having on the crowd. Aunt Helen was in on the whole thing and trying not to laugh. Some of the mountain men thought the rumble of laughter was the way the crowd had of reacting to the seriousness and historical authenticity of their many mountain man costumes. Others thought people were a little over-awed by them, impressed to the point where they needed some relief which they had found in a comical clown, perhaps, near them at the sidewalk.

Stephanie marched another block and then dropped a pace behind her grandfather and Helen and waited for another of those miraculous piles of steaming green fun that put everyone in a good mood. When one finally came, she kept her eye on it and maneuvered herself so that she would come straight on to it. That way she could step over the stinking load in an elaborate fashion, which would make more people, new people, laugh. And it did come and she did step and the crowd did laugh at what she did. It was a miracle! She was an entertainer! And with such a simple prop. There seemed to be a lot of it, too. Grandpa had said she should be the star of the parade.

And another pile came! She jumped over that gob of horse poop like a silly lord a-leaping. She flung her body out into space and soared over that glob of gunk like some kind of stupid poopy headed prince who was dreaming of his lady love and full of all kinds of imaginary, princely, poopy thoughts.

Whee!

The crowd loved it.

Stephanie beamed a smug sort of self-satisfied smile and bowed in several directions.

A long stretch without horse poop ensued.

When the mountain man group reached the intersection of Desperation Street and Wreckage Avenue, she thought it would be funny to scratch her underarms like a little silly monkey. And people liked that a lot, too.

Then she tried hopping instead of walking. Lots of the kids thought that was very funny and laughed and laughed.

The marching men began to notice and look around and so she stopped all her crazy antics for a while and walked soberly looking around as though she was uncertain what was making all the people in the crowd laugh. Who did they think they were laughing at when mountain men were so awfully serious and all?

After that, she walked behind Grandpa Drummond. It only took her a few minutes and she was pulling a hundred different faces. She puffed out her cheeks and crossed her eyes. She scratched her belly and picked at her bottom in a goofy way, lifting her legs and seeming to scratch her crack in an excruciating fashion.

She then decided that it would be humorous to stride down the street with her legs wide apart while walking on the sides of her feet. The crowd liked this quite a bit and lots of people were tittering at the girl walking in a crazy way.

For a while she decided to march like a wind-up toy and she buzzed around a new pile of horse pooh.

She reached to the back of her pants and pretended to give herself a wedgie and then chased a Sabar clown in a dinky car.

That was when the crowd went wild and Mr. Thom turned around to see exactly what all the commotion was about. He looked directly at her as she was crossing her eyes and puffing out her cheeks. She expelled air and smiled in a sickly fashion at him.

"Hi, Mr. Thom," she called.

* * *

The parade was over.

She had loved the whole thing, except for the part when Mr. Thom had squeezed her neck. That hurt and she told Mr. Thom that it did but he didn't stop what he was doing and he wouldn't take his hands off her neck as he propelled her toward the curb. Mr. Thom's face went sort of purplish and he told Aunt Helen that she'd better stop Stephanie from behaving silly for the rest of the parade for, "God save my soul, I want to kill her."

It was news to Stephanie that God was a woman, but if Mr. Thom said so, she would have to believe him, however, killing God, if God were a man or a woman, would not be a good idea, Stephanie reckoned. A person could get into a lot of trouble for doing something like that.

It was Sunday noon, the day after the parade, and Aunt Helen and Stephanie lay flat on their backs in the grass near the koi fountain in Grandpa Drummond's garden. An early hint of summer's warmth replaced the cold wind that had blown all night Thursday and all day Friday, when Helen had walked around the backyard with a sour look on her face and Stephanie had been afraid to go out to play with her. The two of them now were able to bask on the sunny green carpet, though the grass did feel a little damp on their backs if they lay in one place too long. From their reclining positions, the desert sky was so blue, so endlessly blue, and whenever Aunt Helen sat up, she liked noticing the way it crowned the crumbled gray and lavender mountains with their high saddles and rocky cliffs.

Stephanie noticed that Aunt Helen had been sighing frequently since they had been out lounging in the grass. Stephanie didn't know it, but the sounds Helen was making were sighs of contentment, full of understanding of her new relationship with the world.

By the end of the parade late on Saturday, Aunt Helen's mood had begun to soar. Helen approved of the way Stephanie had handled Mr. Thom; it was great fun seeing him turn purple. Helen felt she was glimpsing creative freedom in her niece. Stephanie's irrepressible spirit encouraged her aunt to think that it might be possible for her to paint without listening to the critic. She only hoped —and the news was promising--that Mr. Thom wouldn't succeed in his efforts to removed Grandpa Drummond from the Mountain Man Club. Her father was spending a few hours on the phone making sure Mr. Thom didn't get his way.

Some of Stephanie's creative acts at her grandparents' mansion had been discovered earlier that Sunday morning, but neither Drummond nor Hilda could conceive of their curator-granddaughter making the messes. Drummond surmised that a bug had eaten the cocoons off the belt and planned on having the entire house fumigated as soon as possible, which might help with the moth-eaten trophy heads, also. Drummond and Hilda imagined that the elk head had fallen on its own and the force had knocked out the lion's eye. Drummond recorded a message for Dr. Adobe asking him for an estimate to mend the library wall and he planned to get estimates for repairs from a wallpaper hanger, too. Because he never really examined his art closely, he failed to notice the boy in the oil painting scribbled in with permanent marker.

Aunt Helen, her head on the grass that Sunday noon, turned to look into the deep shade of a nearby bush. She frowned at what she saw. How had two of her father's most valuable pots arrived underneath a shrub along with the skull of a beaver? Helen thought for a moment and then realized that Stephanie had told her there was a skull she wanted to bury; Helen figured that must be it. Sometime later that afternoon, Helen decided, the valuable pots crammed with flowers and wet beans would have to be washed and set back carefully on their shelf.

"Do you know something?" asked Aunt Helen, philosophically as she turned away from the bush and gaped lazily at the sky. She didn't complete her rhetorical question but left it dangling.

"What?" asked Stephanie dutifully, after a

minute's lag.

Aunt Helen told Stephanie that there was something she had always wanted to do that wasn't painting and it was something Stephanie and she could do together.

"Hmmm," said Stephanie, mulling over interesting activities that she had contemplated so far in her life, "Did you maybe want to own a baby snake and put a teeny bonnet on it?"

"No," said Aunt Helen thoughtfully, and she raised one finger from her hands that folded over her chest. For a second, she remained stymied as to the best reply to her niece. "Stephanie, I've never wanted to do that. That's a very odd thing to want to do, actually. It worries me that you would want to bother a snake that way."

"Why, what do you mean 'bother'?" asked Stephanie adopting her aunt's high degree of astonishment.

"Well, that's not respecting the animal, putting a bonnet on it, but let's don't get distracted. No, what I've wanted, what I've always wanted when I lived at this house, I should say, besides being able to paint all the time, as you know, was to see if I could take a sip, or even a big drink, out of one of those black O'odham baskets which Grandpa Henry bought on the reservation. The two in the bottom of the big green bookcases near the front door."

Stephanie stared long and hard at her aunt to try to figure out what she was up to. This secret ambition struck her as stupid. She couldn't see the thrill in it. Then, suddenly, she grabbed her elbows and hugged herself tightly. Her eyebrows rose and she sucked in her breath dramatically. "Aunt Helen," said Stephanie slowly, "Are those black baskets poisoned?"

Aunt Helen frowned. "No, no they're not. It's just devil's claw that makes the black baskets black. They used devil's claw instead of soaptree yucca. It's supposed to be waterproofing. The O'odham wash their dishes in big old black baskets. They don't think they're sacred or anything. I've always wanted to try drinking out of one to see if they're really waterproof. Do you see what I mean?"

"But Aunt Helen," Stephanie said ominously, "devil's claw sounds a lot like a poison, don't you think? You know—a devil's claw. Get it? The claw of a devil?"

"No...it isn't poison," Aunt Helen protested. She stopped talking and thought about this for a while. Of course, she knew very well that devil's claw wasn't poisonous, but what good was it to insist on the mundane truth and what fun it would be to pretend! "Well," said Aunt Helen cautiously but with a small amount of fun creeping into her voice, "it would be a dangerous thing to attempt, but couldn't we see if see they are poisoned?"

"Honestly?"

"Yes. Let's get those two. Near the front door. Two big black baskets," said Helen.

Stephanie stood up and started to run. She stopped before she had gone a few steps. "But wait. What do you think we ought to drink in them?"

"I'll have a root beer," said Helen, "You get what you want. Out of the refrigerator. Don't let anyone stop you."

"I'm gonna get the same. Root beer," said Stephanie happily.

Stephanie turned and darted inside. She took a path through the old house that led directly to the low bookshelf, which she remembered because she had gotten the turquoise rocks off the skull there late Friday night. The black baskets were displayed on small stands, the centers of the baskets cupped toward each other. She nested them together and scrambled away to the kitchen.

She pulled the refrigerator door open and picked out two root beer cans. As she ran back outside, the frosty cans conked against each other in the center of the top basket.

"Perfect," said Aunt Helen when Stephanie reemerged. "I shall prepare the potions for us."

Helen sat cross-legged and Stephanie

imitated her. Helen put the baskets side-by-side and popped open the first can.

Ever so carefully, tilting the can gently, she poured the bubbly brown brew into one basket. She popped open the other can and filled the other basket.

Helen held her basket up in the air and checked the bottom.

"Is it holding? Look underneath," asked Stephanie, "We don't want our poison running out."

"Yes, it is holding," said Helen. "We'll give the poison time to get into the root beer, if it's going to."

Helen placed her basket on the grass again. The black root beer bubbled merrily in the basket.

"Is that enough time?" asked Stephanie.

"Yeah, I guess so," said Helen.

"Now, now, we drink our poison," said Stephanie solemnly. "Life has been pretty good, maybe okay, but time for poison anyway."

"Sure," said Aunt Helen.

"To our poison," said Stephanie.

"To our poison!" cried Aunt Helen.

Stephanie picked up the basket and tilted some into her mouth. She held the root beer in her mouth while Helen grabbed her black basket and quaffed from the edge.

Stephanie swallowed. "Down the hatch!"

Stephanie said after she had swallowed, remembering a pirate's line.

"The hatch," said her aunt.

"Look at that," said Helen, lifting his basket above her head to examine the dry bottom, "it's really good. We'll wash them out later with the hose."

"But I'm not dying," Stephanie said, slightly put out.

"Neither am I!" said Aunt Helen happily. "Oh God, neither am I! Today I am most definitely not dying, Stephanie. And first thing tomorrow I'll finally start my first really great painting. I'll be painting the pictures I've always seen in my head. And I'm not worried about doing well. I'm not judging the work. I'm just going to do them the way they turn out. The way they become will be the way they are supposed to be. Isn't it fabulous and fun? Isn't it great that today we don't have to die?"

Stephanie smiled and hugged her aunt. "Yeah, Aunt Helen, it's really great," she was hanging on her aunt's neck. "And you know something...I really like you."

"Thank you."

"I mean really, you know."

"Oh, I know."

"Aunt Helen, when are we going to bury the skull that I found in Grandpa Drummond's house?"

"Now! I forgot! We'll have a ceremony. Definitely, but wait! Wait here!" Helen leapt up and ran into the house.

Stephanie had almost grown tired of waiting for Aunt Helen when an astonishing and horrible figure flung open the French doors and dashed across the lawn toward her. This figure was shaking its legs and wiggling its hips and yes, hooting wildly like some kind of banshee. The figure was wearing that terrifying Mexican mask, the one with the stringy black hair that Stephanie had used to frighten her aunt in bed.

As the horrid thing got closer to an increasingly startled Stephanie, it was Aunt Helen's voice that suddenly cried, "Now it is time! Time for that wonderful burial!"

And so, it was time, their special time together, a time they never forgot.

❈ ❈ ❈

But as the world will have it, later times came also. Stephanie's parents took her home that night and Stephanie slept in her own bed. She absconded with *Terror Tales* in her little suitcase without her grandparents' permission. Their neighbor, Mrs. Webster, revealed that she was surprised, but glad, to see them back alive on Monday morning, but she hoped Stephanie's parents would consider themselves lucky and never venture south of the border again.

And Helen was all right. Uncle Will came to pick her up on Monday morning and found her worlds better mentally, a feat she always attributed to her short weekend spent in the company of her uninhibited, eight-year-old niece.

BOOKS BY THIS AUTHOR

Juan And Willy

Who hasn't dreamed of finding gold? When Juan and Willy are fired from their jobs as car handlers at a dealership, a desire for gold possesses them. Locating a lost mine, however, means they have to outsmart a kid, a huge challenge for this pair. With an idea of where some lost gold might be, they search for a truck with an intact transmission that isn't full of feral cats. Of course, abandoned mines aren't safe places either, a fact especially true for these sorry, but sweet, friends.

Trombones Can Laugh

Circuses and parades go wildly awry when James Sauerbaugh joins a band of Shriners as a substitute trombonist. The band members are ancient and drunk out of their minds, but James comes to relish the friendships and wild fun on the bus and on parade floats. When Moses Grand, a fellow trombonist, rescues him from death at the hands of a ruthless killer, the story takes a dark turn. Nobody can have enough books with circuses and parades in them.

Familiar Artifacts

Attention, suspense fans! In this collection of strange tales you will watch in horror as phosgene gas creeps toward the Arizona boosters who've done something truly shocking at their World War I training camp. You will shop--if you dare--at the weird store of an asthmatic witch who likes to summon dead relatives for her customers. You will commiserate with a hunter so distracted by learning about animal tracks that he loses track of his girlfriend. You will fend off a strange puppeteer, and journey along with a substitute teacher on her disconcerting day spent caring for a violent and abused boy. Did he really describe a murder? Twelve anomalous short stories are specially crafted to jolt you out of the mundane. Proceed with caution!

Last Days In The Desert

A wild party leads to a day of hungover misadventures for three undergrads who had hoped to shut down their rental house and get back their security deposit before leaving town. Instead they have to fix a gaping hole in an adobe wall and rid themselves of unwanted graduation "presents," both the result of the uproarious party. A zany romp of high and low comedy.

Genuine Aboriginal Democracy

Delve into twelve quirky tales. Flee to a reservation with a persecuted professor of archaeology. Snuggle kittens at a consciousness raising under the critical eye of a crabby host. Freeze in place as rattlesnakes slither across the field at a scout gathering. Evade a demented stalker on the first day of work at a new job. Short fiction finely wrought for your reading pleasure.

CONNECT WITH LORRAINE RAY

Read her Smashwords interview at https://www.smashwords.com/interview/LoRay and pose questions.

Email: lorraine.ray00@gmail.com

Contact her on Twitter: http://twitter.com/@LoRay00

ABOUT THE AUTHOR

Lorraine Ray

Visit amazon.com/author/lorraine-ray for many more books! Get boring details about this obscure author!

Made in the USA
Las Vegas, NV
24 January 2024

84858601R00073